MURDER MAKES THE MARE GO

MURDER MAKES THE MARE GO

JACK DOLPH

COACHWHIP PUBLICATIONS
Greenville, Ohio

To Peter who, on reading the manuscript, said . . . "Hey! You know, it's not bad at all for just have been written around home like that!"

First published 1950
John ("Jack") Mather Dolph, 1895-1962
CoachwhipBooks.com

ISBN 1-61646-500-X
ISBN-13 978-1-61646-500-1

1

The death of Snuffy Goddard, an obscure person, from obscure causes, in an obscure basement room in Harker Street, sounded only a piping requiem against the diapason of the city's living.

The little man did receive in death, however, certain attentions which were rather more important than anything that had happened to him in life, for he twice achieved the notice of the civil authorities, the newspapers, and the actuaries of the insurance companies.

In his first contact with these agencies, the proceedings were marked by a disinterested and impersonal quality which would have disappointed Goddard, who loved a word of approval from his betters. The authorities accepted his undersized remains, held them for the required period, and buried them, finally, in the space allotted by the county for such persons. The newspapers disposed of the matter with an agate line. The actuaries received the news without enthusiasm—since the deceased had chucked it at the routine age of fifty-eight, adding nothing to man's hope of longevity.

It is possible that one of these latter gentlemen may have raised an eyebrow on noting the stated cause of death. In these days of the sulfa drugs and penicillin, a fatal septicemia could rate a second glance, even among the uninsured.

I hadn't known the man and didn't know anybody who had. As a matter of fact, except for a series of circumstances which fell, almost casually, into place, Snuffy might have continued to rest in whatever peace he could find in his pauper's grave. The way it turned out, I got to know him very well indeed.

The civil authorities came to know him, too, along with the newspapers and the actuaries. It was they who joined in awarding him, at last, the recognition he deserved—a proper send-off during which Snuffy was permitted to return for several busy days among the living to impart the information he had carried with him to the potters' field—the fact that he had been murdered.

I include all this because, for several weeks this spring, Snuffy's wraith hung over my shoulder at meals, disturbed my sleep, and annoyed hell out of me in general.

It was this way . . .

I don't know how many times the telephone had rung. I answered it without turning on the bedstand light. The cutting tenseness of the man's voice woke me thoroughly.

"Doc Connor?"

"Speaking."

"Listen, Doc, this is Tom Bradford. Can you come out right away?"

"Wait till I shake my head a couple of times, Tom." Bradford is a running-horse trainer I've known casually for a couple of years. "Okey. Now tell me again."

"There's been some trouble out here, Doc, and I couldn't think of anybody to call but you."

"Somebody hurt?"

"No. It's something else."

"What time is it?"

"Close to six. I'm sorry as hell to bother you so early but this thing's got me half crazy. Do you think you could make it?"

"Why—I suppose so, Tom. Do I bring my bag?"

Bradford hesitated a moment. "Damned if I know. I hadn't thought about it. Maybe you'd better, at that."

"Is there some reason you can't tell me about it now?"

"I don't like to. I'm using the public phone in the track kitchen—you know how that is." I could hear the banging of dishes and the murmur of men's voices. Half the back-side population of the track would be having breakfast. "It's something I wouldn't want to get around, Doc."

"I'll be right out."

"I'd sure appreciate it. Do you mind taking a cab from the subway? I don't think I'd better leave the barn any more until—later."

"That's all right, Tom. See you in around forty minutes."

I threw on some clothes, wondering what had upset the guy so badly. The little I'd seen of him had given me the impression he was pretty easygoing—a soft-spoken Georgia man who drawled the name of his home state into something rhyming with dowager. Bradford had ten or twelve horses for several owners and was recognized as a good trainer. His father, old Lance Bradford, had been one of the best in the business.

It was getting light when I turned out of Forty-eighth Street and headed across Broadway to the subway. March was going out like a lamb and the clean smell of the air reminded me that they'd be off and running around town in two weeks or so. That's for me.

I suppose Tom Bradford thought of that when he called me. It's common knowledge in our neighborhood that anything having to do with racing supersedes practically everything else in my unorthodox life. People take it for granted that I'm happier when one of my trainer friends consults me about a popped osselet than when I'm laboring diligently—as I do twice a week—with my strictly non-paying medical practice.

As I climbed out of the subway and dumped my tools into a cab, I decided that, whatever Tom wanted of me that morning, it wouldn't be to look at an osselet.

The guard at the back-side gate said, "Hi, Doc, you're rushin' the season a little, ain't ya?"

We eased along the familiar way. The warming breeze brought the odors of earth, clean manure, timothy, and the bright pungence of wood smoke from the water heaters. The sun slanted pleasantly across the long rows of white barns, set the infield dew to glistening, and pointed to the red and gold of the quarter poles.

A few early sets were galloping on the track and their hoofbeats drummed in steady rhythm to their breathing.

A boy cantered a playful yearling along the outside rail—singing the off-key lullaby that is often the trademark of a good hand with the young ones. The colt had turned his ears back to listen.

I sent the cab away at Bradford's barn and walked over to the shed. A set was ready to go out and Tom was giving instructions. When he saw me coming he sent the horses out and hurried over to meet me.

"By God, Doc, you were swell to come out." He took my bag and set it on the tack-room bunk. "I've got some real nasty trouble here and I know you're going to feel the same way I do about it. I think you're going to want to help me out."

"Of course I will, Tom—if I can. Tell me about it."

"There ain't anything to tell. Come over here and have a look." He led me to what had seemed to be an empty stall and opened the half door. On the bright straw bed lay a horse. "There she is, Doc. I want to know what you think."

It was a bay filly and she was dead. The morning came into her stall and colored her glossy red-brown coat. I touched her side. It was cool and stiff. The bedding was undisturbed. She hadn't threshed around. She'd simply lain down. I turned to Bradford and he was staring dismally at a halter and shank which lay on the ground in front of the stall.

"How long has she been dead, Tom?"

"She was dead when the watchman set the feed tubs in this morning at four-thirty. He called me."

"I take it for granted you think her death wasn't caused by heart failure—like it looks." The filly showed no sign of external injury.

"That's right." Bradford touched the halter with his foot. "She was tied at some time during the night, Doc. You know where the halters and shanks are kept at night in any racing barn. Yesterday evening when we left, that halter was hanging on this door and the shank was rolled and slung under it. This morning they were on the ground there where you see them."

"What about the watchman? Wasn't he around all night?"

"Yes. He was around. He's a good man. The trouble is t that, in the off season, like now, when there's no racing at the track, we share a watchman with the Starrett people over in 5-A. The man is away from our horses for twenty, thirty minutes or so at a time. He usually eats his lunch around midnight in their tack room, too, because they've got an electric plate he can heat his coffee on."

I looked across the way and saw 5-C. "The Starrett barn would be directly behind us then."

"That's right. The man can't see this side from over there." Bradford shuffled his feet and looked miserable. "It isn't the best arrangement in the world, but hell, how often would you expect this sort of thing to happen?"

"You wouldn't." I took another look at the filly—turned her cold eyelids back and sniffed at her delicate nostrils for evidence of some recognizable drug. Her water bucket was half full and had no unusual odor or taste. She'd been a handsome little thing—with a solid, well-muscled body, good bone, and a dainty head. I walked out of the stall and closed the half door behind me. "You said anything to anyone else about this, Tom?"

"No."

I looked down the shed where several ginnies were mucking out the stalls of the set which was working on the track. I recognized old Pop Asher, whom I'd seen around for years. Pop had been with the horses all his life.

"What about the ginnies?"

The man looked down the shed. There was no talk down there—none of the stall-to-stall wisecracks and chatter that are as much a part of a ginny as his rub rag. "The boys think it was heart failure."

"What about the halter and shank?"

Tom grinned sadly. "I was here before they came. They think I tried to pull the mare's head up—that I thought she might have been alive." He headed for the tack room. "Let's go in here where we can sit down."

I moved my bag and sat on the bunk. Bradford lit a cigarette and slumped into a chair. He took his hat off and mussed his crisp, dark hair. "Doc, what kind of a rotten son would hate me bad enough to do a thing like that to a fine race mare?"

"Hate you or maybe somebody else. Who'd she belong to?"

"Rick Fogan. Know him?"

"To speak to—that's about all." Fogan owned a place called the Ricky Club—a big nitery where the food was not too bad and the show fair as a rule. "I'd heard he'd bought some horses."

"I've got seven head for him now. He bought this filly out of New Orleans—shipped her here a little over three weeks ago." The man pulled himself off his chair and stood with his back to me in the doorway.'

"You say she was a good-quality race mare?"

He turned and handed me a card he'd been crumpling in his hand. He'd taken it from its small frame tacked alongside the stall door. It read, "ARMADA, b.f. 3—Bridgedeck-Spanish Miss."

"She only ran three times last year as a two-year-old and win two of them. One was a stake." Bradford came back and sat down again. "Fogan's got her eligible for a lot of the good filly stakes this year. I don't know what the hell I'm going to tell the guy!"

"I don't wonder, fella, it's a tough spot."

"Tough enough to wash me up as a trainer, Doc. It's a cinch I'll lose the Fogan horses—whether this mare was poisoned or not. If the word gets out, I'll never get another horse."

I began thinking of the people who might want to know more about it. "What about the insurance investigators?"

"There won't be any insurance investigators. Fogan said there'd be time enough for insurance when we got to racing. That makes it worse on him, of course."

"Actually, then, you've got nobody but Fogan to worry about." I thought of the big, tough, quiet man who ran the Ricky Club. He didn't do much talking about anything. You'd hardly pick him to gossip about his misfortunes. It was a long time before Bradford answered.

"Yes. I suppose Fogan's the man who'll have to decide whether I stay in business or not. There's certainly nobody else concerned."

"If it's that way, Tom, why didn't you just call the animal disposal people and let it go at that? Why'd you call me?"

He came up with a punchy grin. I felt sorry as hell for him. "You don't think that idea didn't occur to me, do you, Doc?"

"It damned well would have occurred to me."

"It might have been better all around, but I couldn't get myself to do it that way. I've been with horses a long time—since I was a kid and galloped them for the old man. I like 'em. I know some people in this business that don't, but I do. There's good ones and there's common ones but mostly they do the best they can with what they've got to do it with. I never abused a horse in my life and I've got no use for anybody that does. I called you because I want to lay my hands on the guy that killed that mare."

I felt pretty much that way myself and said so. I guess from the time the Arabs began sharing their dates and milk with their horses at the tent flaps, there's been some sort of a bond. I've had it since the Old Doc gave me my first pony. Neither Bradford nor I said anything for a while. Pop Asher came to the door and asked if the brown colt was to be breezed. Tom told him to put it off till tomorrow.

When he looked back to me he said, "Doc, I can't think of anybody who'd want to do this to me. It's got to be somebody that's trying to hit at Rick Fogan. Either that or a maniac."

"If it was a maniac, he was a smart one."

"What do you mean?"

"The mare was killed painlessly and skillfully. There aren't too many ways to do that."

He got up and we walked down the shed toward the dead mare's stall. "How, for instance?"

We looked at the undisturbed bedding again and the natural, sleeping position of the filly. I said, "If someone gave me one guess, I'd say magnesium sulfate—intravenously."

"It would work that way?"

"Exactly. A solution of ordinary Epsom salts in the blood stream. She'd simply get tired and lie down."

Bradford scratched his head with impatience. "But that would take a veterinarian."

"Not at all." I looked down the shed to where Pop Asher was working. "Almost anybody who'd worked around horses awhile could do it. Take old Pop down there . . ."

"God damn it, Doc, Pop would never do a thing like—"

"Hold it! Keep your hat on! I didn't say he would. I'm simply saying that an old-timer like Pop would know how to find a vein and pump something into it. You haven't got a ginny in the barn that doesn't think he knows more about a horse than any vet."

"That's true, of course." He shook an idea out of his head. "I hate to think of a horseman doing it."

"It wasn't a piano tuner, Tom. This guy knew what he was about. I'm sure that, if he'd had more time, he'd have hung up the halter and rolled the shank and you'd probably have never known the difference." A thought occurred to me that I hadn't considered before. "Unless, of course, he *wanted* Fogan to know that the mare had been killed—a sort of warning or something."

"In that case, it would be better to tell him the truth."

"I think so, Tom. I've got a hunch it wouldn't go any further. The police wouldn't have any interest in this unless Fogan made a complaint. Killing a horse isn't murder. It's vandalism—wanton destruction of property or whatever they call it. Of course it's easy enough for me to advise you what to tell Fogan. I don't lose anything."

"I know." He strode off toward the tack room. "I'll get my coat and drive you to the subway."

I followed him. "Tom."

He turned. "What?"

"Wouldn't you like to know about it—for sure?"

"If it means calling a vet . . ."

I picked my bag off the cot. "It doesn't. I'll do it."

Bradford followed me as I headed toward the stall. When he didn't say anything, I turned and faced him. He looked troubled—

kicked the dirt around to fill a small depression made by the mare's foot the last time she'd stepped out of her doorway. "Do you want to know for sure, Tom?"

"Sure, Doc! Of course I want to know."

I went into the stall as Tom wheeled and walked rapidly down the shed. As a man who's strictly a sucker for a horse, I had a very unpleasant quarter hour.

2

On the way home I stopped by the laboratory and left my specimen. By the time I got to the apartment the office side was full of customers. I walked through the waiting room, said good-morning-all or something and, as tactfully as I could, pulled out a couple of Air-wicks. Forty-eighth and Broadway is definitely not one of the choicer residential areas and my custom of not sending out any bills tends to produce little or no fragrance among the patientry.

A few rugged souls of considerable means have, for some reason, determined to adopt me as their personal physician, and occasionally I find one sitting it out with the rest. I had almost made it through the door to the office before I discovered that we had one aboard. A faint but undeniable trail of scotch whisky followed me and I turned around to track it down.

Danny Marra, the theatrical agent, was sitting in the corner in something of a coma. He looked at me out of a pair of very red eyes and said, "Ah! The good, gray doctor, come to give us health and cheer! I bid you welcome."

I told him to come in and made a small speech to the assembled. "As you know, we usually work on the first-come-first-served basis. This gentleman, however, is one of the faithful sponsors of our clinic, so he will come first this morning. Incidentally, it will cost him ten bucks, so give him a great big hand."

They applauded vigorously. Danny drooped into the office and fell into the big chair. "Doc, please! No gags this morning!"

"What's the trouble, chum?"

The effort of getting into the room had turned him a bit green and I waited until he got his normal pallor back. "I been curing a cold for two days. I got drunk. The cold's gone—but look at me!"

"I do better with hangovers than I do with colds anyway." While I was getting the B1 ampule and the syringe, I said, "By the way, Danny, while I shoot you full of health how about telling me a couple of things?"

"For ten bucks I have to tell you things besides? Like what?"

"Like do you book acts into Rick Fogan's club?"

"Not acts, Doc. I book the line, though. Ten girls."

"Take off your coat and roll a sleeve up. You know Fogan pretty well?"

"Yeah. Pretty well. I get around there quite a lot." He groaned and shaded his eyes from the window. "Why do you ask about Fogan?"

"A friend of mine is doing some horse business with him. I just wondered what sort of a guy he is."

"I never had any trouble doing business with him. Fogan's a good enough joe—tough as hell when he wants to be, but he's all right. He's got horses now, eh?"

"Yeah. A small string. Tell me; what did he used to do in New Orleans? Have you ever heard?"

"He ran a café there too. I think he was in partnership with his present headwaiter."

"Hold your arm still and pump your fist a couple of times. You mean his former partner works for him at the Ricky Club?"

"Something like that—a Frenchman named Lauziere. Ouch!"

"Hold it! That's better. So Lauziere used to be his partner—seems like a funny spot for a guy. What's this Lauziere like?"

"He's strictly a heel. Nasty as hell. I guess you know that the headwaiter at a place like that has quite a lot to do with the show." I told him I didn't. "Well, this guy makes it really tough for the girls. A big smile for the customers and the stars but mean to the kids in the line."

"Probably sore because Fogan's left him behind."

"That could be. It might account for a lot of the things he does. Fogan doesn't front for the place very much and Lauziere really takes over. You'd think he owned the joint instead of Rick."

"Here. Put your finger on this. Do you know if Lauziere has ever been around the horses?"

"He must have. His office is full of pictures of them. That's one of the things that makes the girls so sore. He's got an office full of horse pictures but if anybody tries to use the phone to play one, he raises hell."

"A vicious character."

"You aren't just kidding!" The guy stared at me. "Hey! You know, Doc? I can taste the stuff!"

"That's swell. I must have got it in the right place. Thanks for telling me about Fogan and Lauziere. The nick is ten."

"I oughtta call the cops!" He dug around and came up with a bill. "If I ever get sick with anything respectable, I'm going to my wife's doctor."

He started toward the door, leaned against the jamb, and started to laugh. "You know, Doc, I just thought of a helluva gag! It goes like this. You soak me ten bucks for your charity patients, see? Then I say, 'Who do you think you're Robin'? Hood?'" He giggled until his hangover caught up with him again, and left.

I put the ten in an old cigar box I use for such boodle and pushed the buzzer which starts the morning rat race.

Sometime around noon the laboratory called. ". . . definite indications of magnesium sulfate, Doctor. Shall I go ahead with the quantitative?"

"I don't think so, Harry. Any of the stuff is too much. No, let it go and bill me when you send your findings."

When I'd seen the last patient on his way I sat at my desk for a long time thinking about the dead filly, Armada. Her killing seemed an act of pure viciousness. It could hardly have happened during the racing season when the track would be completely patrolled, day and night—and when, perhaps, there might have been some unpleasant reason for her destruction.

That sort of thing doesn't happen in racing any more. Even the oldest of racing's sins—doping—has been reduced to almost nothing and the cause of most of it, the gangster-gambler, is usually chucked out of the park on sight.

I wondered about Fogan's owner's license. You can't own race horses these days, unless you can present a clean bill of health to the associations. At least you can't race them. The Ricky Club drew, among its rather large patronage, some wrong people and, whether Fogan wanted them there or not, they came, sat, and were seen. I felt certain that the owner of Armada had been subjected to a searching examination before he was granted a license to race his horses.

Tom Bradford called about three and I told him the mare had been poisoned.

"Fogan's coming to see you, Doc."

"You told him the truth?"

"Yes."

"How did he take it?"

Bradford hesitated. "I'm damned if I know. He didn't say anything—just listened. I talked to him on the phone about half an hour ago. Couldn't reach him before. I asked him if he wanted to come out before I sent the mare away and he said it wasn't necessary."

"No talk of the police?"

"No talk of anything. He just thanked me and hung up."

The buzzer sounded from below. "Well, keep your tailboard up, kid, I think your boss is arriving right now. I'll see you—call you if I learn anything."

"Thanks, Doc. My home phone's in the Queens book."

I punched the latch button and waited for the clumping of the elevator to stop. Then he stood in the door—a tall man, lean without seeming thin, powerful without seeming heavy. He was probably crowding forty-five. For a long, awkward moment each of us waited for the other to say something. I had the feeling that it was his silence, not mine. That annoyed me.

"Dr. Connor?"

"Yes. Will you come in?"

"Thank you. I think I would have recognized you." He stepped easily into the room and looked around. "I'm Rick Fogan."

His voice was very quiet, his gray eyes flanked by high cheekbones which looked scrubbed. I offered him a chair. "I think I would have recognized you, too."

"I've seen you at the club. It always creates a stir among the—younger people of our group."

"I hadn't realized I'd become so notorious. Will you have a drink?"

The man put a very expensive hat carefully on the floor and manufactured a smile for me. "No, thank you. I've contrived to sell a great deal of liquor in my life without learning to drink it. Please have one yourself, though." He relaxed in his chair and studied my horse pictures. "Your quarters are very pleasant, Doctor."

"Thanks. I'm pretty well dug in here." I poured myself a modest Old Forester and water, sat down, and waited the guy out. He seemed in no hurry as he watched me sip some of my drink. After a while he leaned forward with his elbows on his knees.

"Doctor, I understand Tom Bradford called you out to the track this morning."

"That's right. He did. I felt very sorry for him when I found out what had happened. It was a tough break."

"Yes. It was a tough break for Tom." He worked up another smile of sorts. "Perhaps you even recognized that it was a tough break for me too."

I sensed his hardness and his assurance. If I'd known he was a right guy I'd have been a lot more comfortable. As it was, I took refuge in my Forester. When I'd swallowed, I said:

"Of course. On the other hand, you lose a horse. Bradford loses his reputation—or stands to lose it."

"That's quite true." He lit a cigarette, then looked at it curiously, as though he hadn't expected to find it in his hand. "Tell me. What makes you think the filly was—purposefully destroyed?"

"The best evidence in the world—an analysis of her blood. I got word from the laboratory this afternoon. She was, as you say, purposefully and skillfully destroyed."

Fogan deliberated for some time. "How did it happen?"

I did a little deliberating myself. "Someone who had knowledge of the movements of the watchman went into her stall with a prepared solution of magnesium sulfate in a syringe. He could have carried it anyplace. It didn't have to be sterile. There was one light burning in front of the tack room which wouldn't have done him much good—so he probably carried a small flashlight. It was as simple as that. He found a vein—I didn't bother to look for the puncture—inserted the needle, and pressed the plunger. It could have been accomplished in half the time the watchman took for his lunch."

"But he left no evidence of all this." Fogan was definitely not smiling now.

"That's true, Fogan. The only way we'll find him is to figure out what friend of yours—with a rather specialized knowledge of horses—could have disliked you enough to do this to you."

"I think you said, 'We'll find him,' didn't you, Doctor?"

"Yes. I think that's what I said. Why?"

"May I digress? So long as Bradford found it necessary to call anyone about the death of my mare before he called me, I'm rather glad he decided on you."

"Why do you say that?"

"Because I feel that you will understand my position in the matter as well as you understand his." He said it simply and without doing any selling.

"Just what is your position in the matter, Fogan?"

"It's simple enough. That's what I came here to explain, as a matter of fact. It's been a number of years since I've run any horses, Doctor—not since the days before an owner was required to secure a license. When I bought this small string I was apparently investigated very thoroughly. The fact that I own and operate a night club, rather than a more conservative business, didn't help my cause any, I feel sure. Toward the end of the investigation period I was even asked some rather pointed questions concerning the ownership of the Ricky Club—with frank reference to certain of my patrons."

I was getting a little tired of the smooth dialogue.

". . . and did you find the investigation offensive, Fogan?"

"Offensive?" I thought he'd flared up for a moment. His gray eyes challenged me. "Why should I have found it offensive, Doctor? I heartily approved of it. I can be fond of racing, too, you know." He surprised me with a comparatively real smile; "There are quite a number of people whose money I take at the Ricky Club that I'd hate to see own race horses."

That made a lot of sense, so I shut up. Fogan carefully crushed the butt of one cigarette and lit another.

"The fact that I was granted my owner's license seems proof enough of my good faith. To be quite frank, I was flattered as hell. There is a certain amount of gambling to be found in my public record—never, however, concerned with horses. It's almost inevitable in the operation of clubs. Now I've got a small string of young horses and a license to race them. I'd like to keep it that way." He leaned back again in his chair. "This is a hell of a start!"

"Especially if some depraved character is running around loose with the fixed idea of killing your horses."

"You know as well as I do that I can't afford a scandal right now." He hesitated, almost shyly. "That, of course, is why I came here this afternoon—to ask your co-operation."

"In helping find the man who killed your mare, Rick?" I guess I must have softened it up with some sort of a grin. He took it easily enough.

"I'm afraid not, Doc. I have reason to believe there will be no further trouble at the barn. I also have . . ."

"Why do you think you won't have any more trouble at the barn?"

Fogan placed his fingertips precisely together and studied them as he answered. "I have sent a very competent man to the track who will act as watchman, for one thing."

". . . and for another thing?"

He laughed aloud. It was hearty and genuine. "I can understand some of the things I've heard about your success as an amateur detective, Doc. You're certainly persistent."

"Look, Rick; I haven't any desire to poke my nose into your affairs and I understand that a public investigation of this thing might be embarrassing—both to you and Tom Bradford. At least give me credit for that much judgment." I found myself on my feet making gestures with my drink. I sat down. "I still don't like people who slaughter horses."

"So you propose to find the man who slaughtered my horse?"

"I propose to try."

The gray eyes studied me very carefully for a moment. After a while Fogan let his breath out slowly and stood up.

"You don't leave me much of a choice, Doc."

"I hadn't intended it that way. I simply—"

"Regardless of how you intended it, I'm convinced that you're going to dig around in some things that could blow up in your, face—and mine. That's a pretty frank statement. Equally frankly, I don't like it at all."

If he was angry, I couldn't find it in his face. He seemed, rather, to be weighing the matter without emotion. I couldn't think of anything that needed saying. Fogan leaned down and picked up his hat before he spoke again.

"Between an investigation which could, accidentally, become public and one which can be conducted strictly privately, I must choose the lesser evil." He held out his hand. "Can you come over to the club tonight?"

"I'd like to."

"Do, then. Ask for me when you first come in. Perhaps you'll honor us by bringing the lovely Miss Storm."

"Thanks. Perhaps I shall."

As I dialed Katie's number I was trying to decide whether Fogan's conversation made sense or whether I was running into an extremely polite but explosive booby trap.

3

A dark little man in a well-cut dinner jacket and an amazingly clean shirt met us at the door of the Ricky Club. He bowed professionally. I started to ask for Rick, only to discover that the thing had been set up like pins in a bowling alley.

"Good evening, Miss Storm—Dr. Connor. Mr. Fogan has asked me to show you to his office." He made a gesture and paraded ahead of us across the foyer.

The queen-of-love-and-beauty took off after him. As I caught up with her, she said, "Who's Mr. Fogan?"

"Rick Fogan. He owns the place."

"That's nice." Then one of those quick takes of hers—strictly katiebusiness. "Or is it?"

"Not very. Tell you about it later."

"Who's the little man?"

"I think his name's Lauziere—the headwaiter. There's a story about him too."

We popped around a musty corner on the side of the building. Katie said, "When do people start shooting each other?"

"Come to think of it, I'm not quite sure. Why?" Lauziere stopped at a door and rapped. Katie grinned at me. "Because, darling, nothing but people shooting each other or horses would have dragged you into the place. See?"

I saw.

Rick Fogan came to the door. "Come in. It's very pleasant to have you." I introduced him to Katie. "I thought we might have a cocktail here before you go to your table."

A waiter appeared and we decided on martinis. Fogan and Katie talked about why he didn't have chromium in his office like night-club owners in the movies. I looked at pictures—performers, horses, and other reminiscent keepsakes. One of the pictures was a building with a large sign reading, "Café Lauziere."

When the cocktails had come and we'd settled down, Fogan pulled a piece of torn newspaper from his pocket and handed it to me.

"I thought you'd be interested, Doctor. It's from tonight's *Form*."

Under "New York Briefs" I read, "Trainer Tom Bradford reports the death, from heart failure, of Richard S. Fogan's promising filly, Armada. The fleet daughter of Bridgedeck-Spanish Miss won two of her three races as a two-year-old and had been entered in several of the important stakes events for her sex this season."

I was glad that Katie, over my shoulder, said, "Oh, what a pity! You must feel terribly about it, Mr. Fogan."

At least the guy would know that I hadn't begun talking to Katie. He gave me a look of appreciation. "I do, Miss Storm. I am very fond of horses."

Katie looked at the clipping again. "Don't I know Tom Bradford, Jimmy?"

(My name's James Cardigan Connor, in case you wondered.)

"Yes. I think you met him once at the track. He's the one—"

"I know. With the wonderful Southern accent—Gowaga . . ."

There was a firm knock at the door. Rick Fogan stepped over and opened it. I heard him say, "Oh. Come in, Rita."

A rich, throaty contralto said, "Sorry, Rick! I didn't know you had guests." Not hoity-toity contralto. The impressive kind.

Rick was murmuring things about wanting her to meet us as he led Rita in by the hand. He did the introductions the hard way—like he'd been reading the book. You could tell she occupied some very special place in the Fogan scheme of things. As to how good-looking she was, I can best describe her by saying that she was fairly tall, redheaded, and that Katie, herself the most beautiful woman God ever made, bristled all over after one look.

Her name was Rita Ross . . . Miss.

Fogan steered her over to us and sat her down near Katie. "You'll hear Rita sing tonight—it's a treat, I assure you." For the first time I saw genuine expression in the gray eyes. "We're very proud of her."

Rita gurgled or something and we all murmured stuff about we were sure they were. You know how those things go. Rick and I beamed across the room while the girls sized each other up. The Ross woman was saying:

"Rick is so extravagant!" She smiled over at him. She had nice teeth. "I think I should remind you, dear, that Katie Storm, here, sings for more people every day than I do in a year. She's a radio celebrity. Tell me! Was 'Recipes-in-Rhythm' your own idea?"

Katie has nice teeth too. She bared 'em. "Yes—fortunately. It had always seemed to me that the home economics programs were pretty dull. I've just tried to lighten mine up a little."

"Well, you've certainly succeeded! You should listen to her sometimes, Rick. She's wonderful!"

The tall man smiled. "I do."

Rita said, "Oh?" Then nobody said anything. Then everybody said things all at once. Then I laughed—which was a mistake. The head of flaming red hair turned deliberately toward me and the cold blue eyes froze me to my chair.

Katie said, "I keep wondering if we haven't met before, Rita. Perhaps in radio."

The woman, it seemed to me, looked startled for an instant. Then she laughed. "Oh, I think not, Katie. My radio career was very brief indeed. I've always preferred to work before an audience."

I thought it was time to do a little ingratiating, so I tossed in that the audience undoubtedly preferred it too. Rick apparently approved of this.

"That's it, Doc. When she sings for radio she leaves half the show in the studio. They're talking television for her now."

From then on, television took the pressure off until Fogan rang for Lauziere to take us to our table. As we trailed him back through the long, twisting hall Katie said, "Brother!"

"No like, eh?"

"I've had pleasanter nightmares." She boomed down the corridor and damned near ran over Lauziere when he stopped at the door of the big room.

"I have taken the liberty of holding a table slightly removed from the ringside, Dr. Connor. It will give you a very good view of the room as well as the show." His dark face was empty, strictly headwaiter.

"Thank you, Lauziere, that'll be very nice."

"I prefer simply Philippe—if you will be so considerate." He turned. "This way, please."

We serpentined through the crowded room to a corner shaded from the general glare by a balcony. The table was of the size they use for four people, pleasantly set for two. There were flowers on it.

Philippe trusted this would be satisfactory, bowed, waved a menu at a waiter, and said, "Perhaps you will give me the pleasure of planning your dinner. There are some things we do not show on the carte . . ."

We told him it sounded wonderful. He headed for the back of the room and disappeared behind the bandstand. The waiter turned up with a wine cooler and set it beside us. Katie said, "What plays? Have you won a radio contest?"

"My darling, I haven't the foggiest idea what plays. All I know is that, no matter how many wine buckets they bring in, we're thoroughly unwelcome guests."

"That's silly—"

"It may sound silly but it isn't. They don't want me around—as a matter of fact, I'm here over Rick Fogan's protest. He's doing a nice job of making the best of it, but he doesn't like it."

"Tell me about it." Katie took a cigarette from the pack I'd shoved out on the table. "Are you in trouble of some kind, Jimmy?"

"I can't tell you about it. Call it for—security reasons. As to whether I'm in trouble, I can't say. Maybe not yet, anyway. I do know one thing, though. There's somebody hereabouts—maybe somebody you met tonight or somebody in this room now—that's scared as hell to see me sitting here."

I held a match for Katie's cigarette. As she looked at me over the flame she said, "Well, here we go again." She got the light and studied the crawling ash. "Another round of cops-'n-robbers!"

"No cops, this time."

"You mean you finally got into trouble all by yourself? No help from Eddie Marsh?"

"That's right. Eddie wouldn't be interested." I didn't mean he wouldn't be interested personally because the big lieutenant of Homicide is as fond of horses as the next man. He just wouldn't be permitted to be interested professionally. Katie looked very serious—and very beautiful—across the table.

The waiter set dishes in front of us. I didn't pay much attention to the pastry shells on them until I dug in and came up with—of all things—an Olympia oyster. I had a sudden rush of memories. Of Hoquiam and Aberdeen. Of the Old Doc and how he loved a Hangtown Fry of these little nuggets of oysterdom. Lauziere noticed and strolled over. "We fly them here by air express. Mr. Fogan is very fond of them." He smiled and went away.

Two newcomers were being seated across the room and the headwaiter hurried over to them. I knew them both by sight—Patsy Dahl and Joe Herrick. As soon as they had given their order Dahl got up and went out toward Fogan's office. Both Dahl and Herrick were the sort of guys you see around all the time—mostly in the lobby of the Garden on fight nights.

Katie put down her fork. "They can fly a lot of those in for my money, They're wonderful!"

"I don't suppose you've ever tasted them before, have you?"

"Never. I've heard about them for years."

While I was telling her about the Olympias the show came on. A spotlight picked up the m.c., and five girls slipped into position in the shadows on each side of the floor. Danny Marra's girls, I remembered. The number one on our side stood almost at our table—a fine-looking woman whose features, on close inspection, told you she'd been around quite a while. When she looked down, I asked her how Danny's cold was.

She laughed. "Pretty well—considering."

"Considering what?"

"Considering how we got it."

"We? Is that nice?"

"Danny thinks so." She hitched up something or other she was wearing. "You see, I'm Maggie Marra."

"You mean that ape keeps you working like this?"

"When he doesn't I'll divorce him. I train these kids and set the floor numbers." The spotlight spread over the room and the band blared a fanfare. "See you around, Doc." Over her shoulder she said, "All right, girls, pick up the tempo from me and for God's sake smile!"

The show was pretty good. Next to closing, Rita Ross did a couple of torchy numbers that were about as well performed as you'll hear in these parts. The customers took it big and hollered for more. She came back and topped the pops with a Victor Herbert standard that showed off a lot of voice.

Katie said, "Whatever else she may be, she can sing."

"Whatever else may she be, darling?"

"For me, she's the Witch of Endor. Jimmy, that woman is just plain no damned good. She gave me the creeps . . . from the first minute I met her." Katie put her hand over her face. I knew she was indulging in what she thinks is a secret habit—holding her nose.

When the lights went up Patsy Dahl had come back to his table. Rick Fogan was on his way toward us. "Better get that expression off your beautiful Irish mug, angel, here comes the light of Rita's life."

Fogan pulled over a chair and sat down. "Are you having a good time?" The waiter wheeled up a table with a spirit lamp and a lot of other paraphernalia on it. "I see that Phil's doing his act for you."

"Superbly!" I watched Lauziere coming toward us with more stuff. "I don't know what's coming up, but it has to be good. My Lord! I haven't tasted an Olympia oyster for years. That was a treat."

"I think this will be pompano. Phil has a way with it." Rick watched Lauziere as he turned up the burner and put two fillets of fish into melted butter. The yellow light flickered against the headwaiter's sharp features. I had the feeling that there was something unpleasant in Fogan's eyes. He leaned toward me and spoke at a level which would make it impossible for Lauziere to hear. "It would be a good idea to be discreet in your table conversation, Doctor. My headwaiter manages to hear a great many things."

"I see. Thanks."

Fogan turned to Katie. "I've asked Rita to join us for a while, Miss Storm. She'll be out as soon as she's changed."

Katie stared resolutely at the flame under the pompano and in an absent sort of voice said, "Then we'll have a chance to tell her how beautifully she sang. She's quite a person, isn't she, Mr. Fogan!"

The tall man said pleasant things about Rita, his eyes on the table across the room where Patsy Dahl and Joe Herrick were sitting. I decided to let the subject alone for the moment, but made up my mind to find out why Rick Fogan chose to do business, in his private office, with wrong people like Dahl.

Lauziere went about his deft business with ritualistic motions. Perhaps Fogan's suggestion had made me over-attentive, but I had the feeling that the little Frenchman was missing nothing. After he had served the pompano he hung around the table for what seemed an extraordinarily long time, taking bows and clearing up the equipment. Strangely enough, when Rita appeared he seemed perfectly contented and sailed off without another glance.

With coffee, Fogan ordered brandy for us—obviously the best in the house. He caught me eying his glass with some suspicion and said, "Apple juice—like the martini I had with you. The service bar gets pretty expert. However, it's the only way I contrive to cheat the customers."

It kept on pretty much like that until the girls went off to fix their faces. Rita offered Katie the facilities of her dressing room and bath and they disappeared behind the bandstand. Fogan moved over and dropped into the chair beside me.

"Doc, between this morning and now, you've seen my whole world. There's actually nothing of any importance in my life which isn't centered right here or at the track—and the track's a pretty new phase, at that. Most of it is under this roof. As I told you this afternoon, I have very strong feelings about any unpleasant—repercussions which might grow out of the mare's death. On the other hand, since you seem to have dealt yourself in, I'm making it my business to see that you get me into as little trouble as possible."

He sat back and lit a cigarette with an impatience that suggested he didn't care too much for the long speech he'd made. I thought it over before I said anything. "By that I suppose you mean that the person I'm looking for will be one of the people in this very small world you've just described."

"I think there's no question about it, Doc. I feel certain that there's not a living soul *outside* that world who cares a damn what happens to me."

". . . and the people *inside* do care a damn what happens to you, Rick?"

"You've seen them. You haven't met all of them, yet, perhaps. But they're all here—the people that love me and the people that hate me."

"Shall we continue to be hypothetical, or may I pry a little?"

Fogan laughed. "You liked those Olympia oysters, Doc—and the pompano?"

"The pompano was beyond imagination, Rick. As for the Olympias, I practically wept into them from homesickness."

"They were a bribe, Doc—a low-down bribe. You're a bought man now, pal."

"So what must I do?"

"So you're free to pry all you want. The bribe is so you'll feel obligated to pry in my presence—or at least to keep me informed where you're doing the prying."

"I need one more assurance before I'll be bought." I thought I might as well give it to him straight.

"What's that?"

"Do you see any reason, as it stands at the moment, why your supervision of my prying may prevent me from finding the person I'm looking for?"

He gave me hard gray eyes. "I'd have no reason to cover for the—" Then, suddenly, he gave me a pair of very gentle ones. "No, Doc, I don't know of any such reason. I don't know anything about it, you see."

"If I'm to get anywhere under this supervised prying system, I have to believe that."

"You can."

"So I pry." I had a feeling the girls would be back any minute and I'd better hurry. "You say that all the people that love you—and hate you—are either here or at the race track."

"That's right. I'm sure of it."

"Would you mind calling off the top name on each list?"

"You've seen it all tonight—Rita—Lauziere . . ."

"If Lauziere hates you, why does he work with you?"

"He's money-hungry. He makes more here than he could possibly earn anywhere else. He would have been a full partner in this business if he hadn't lost his nerve when things were bad. I put my last dime into the deal and I'm winning my bet. Phil's never forgiven me. He hates me and, what's more important, he hates himself for working with me."

That was when the girls came back and Katie started giving out with light touches about going home. Rita helped by knowing how it was—rehearsal in the morning and all that. Rick offered more brandy, which we refused, and Lauziere, with a delicate precision of operation, moved in to see that we damned well got going.

In the cab on the way home Katie was distrait and more than customarily distant. As we hit Sutton Place She suddenly jumped up and down in the seat and yelled, "I've got it!"

"Got what, sweet?"

"I've finally got it! Jimmy, I've figured out where I've met that woman before—Rita."

"Where?"

"She was singing some kind of a local program when I was horsing around all the small stations looking for a break. I even remember her name—she's changed it."

"What was her name?"

"Marguerite Asher!"

Asher!

4

I had no office hours the next day. In addition, when I got back from breakfast, the place was a shambles. Mrs. Parter was swamping out and Mrs. Parter is not one to shilly-shally. The office was full of buckets and mops and the other rooms full of dirty laundry. There was no peace—or a comfortable chair—to be found anywhere. The next step, I knew from harrowing experience, was the vacuum cleaner, so I got out.

Without anything special in mind, I walked up Broadway to Fifty-third where Danny Marra had his office. It's one of those buildings where the lobby is always clattering with kids wearing tap shoes and the elevator is packed with people carrying fiddle cases and trained dogs.

Danny would probably be able to give me a lot more on the Lauziere subject and he might just know something about Rita Asher. There was some sort of a girl in the outer office, but I could see Marra in the back room with his feet on the desk. The telephone rested solidly on his paunch as he talked to somebody. He waved his cigar for me to come in.

". . . look, Maxie, am I a johnny-come-yesterday in this business or something that you should waste my time with such a deal?" I found a chair and put my own feet on the desk. "I get two and a half for the act in the local spots. They got a nice apartment and do their own cooking. Now you want they should go to Miami for a couple of lousy train tickets and three hundred! Go get you some fine acrobats, Max, maybe they can work out their hotel bills as lifeguards." Danny hung up and beamed at me.

"You know Max Finder, Doc?"

"No. What about him?"

"He's one of these guys who's always saying, 'Well, they can't shoot you for trying!' Somebody's going to fool him one of these days." He put the phone back on the desk. "You got something on your mind? Maggie told me she saw you at the club last night."

"Yes. I didn't get much chance to chat with her. You nick Maggie for ten per cent too, Danny?"

"Maggie? Don't be silly. Nobody nicks Maggie for anything. That chorus is her own operation out there—down to the wardrobe. Even that heel, Lauziere, shuts up and listens when she's got something to say."

"Tell me some more about Lauziere. He served our dinner last night. Very fancy."

"He knows his business, all right." Danny hauled his feet off the desk and lit a fresh cigar. "I don't know too much about Lauziere, Doc. Of course there's been some talk around."

"What kind of talk?"

"Oh—the sort you pick up different places. Maggie got some of it from the chef. You have to take it for what it's worth. Seems that Lauziere used to own a pretty prosperous eating place in New Orleans."

"I saw a picture of it in Fogan's office."

"In *Fogan's* office! Seems funny. Well, anyway, the chef said Rick was running a second-rate gambling place around there but he wanted to build up his take. Apparently he went to Lauziere and made some sort of a deal which didn't turn out very well. Whatever happened, it almost broke Lauziere, and Fogan came off with all the chips."

"Fogan says Lauziere lost his nerve—wouldn't continue to put up dough to save the business."

Marra called the girl and signed something. "Whatever it was, Doc, it started a hell of a feud between the partners. Did you hear Lauziere's torch singer last night?"

I thought Danny must be kidding. "*Lauziere's* torch singer! Rita Ross?"

The guy laughed. "That's the crowning touch, I understand. Lauziere picked her up from some local radio station when the Ricky Club was first opened. Brought her along, hired a coach, booked her into the room and, unless there have been some drastic changes made, still takes his cut."

"Ten per cent for Lauziere and the big eyes for Rick Fogan! I'll be damned!" I began to see what Fogan meant when he described the limited world which held his hates and his loves. I wondered, too, about Pop Asher out at the track—quiet old Pop who knew all there was to know about horses. "Is Rita Ross the girl's right name?"

"I guess so. I never heard of any other. First thing anybody in show business knew about her, she was up there singing a hell of a ballad and packin' 'em in," Marra looked over my shoulder through the doorway and said, "Hello, good-lookin'! What got you up so early?" From the outer office Maggie Marra said, "It's my dry-cleaning day. I gotta get out and get all the wardrobe ready to send. Why, hello, Doc. Giving Danny a hypo?" She sailed into the office.

"He's been giving me one this time. I can't quite get over it."

"You can get 'em around here." The phone rang and Danny reached for it. Maggie went on. "Hey, Doc! You can do something for me if you will. I never thought of asking you until last night at the club."

Danny muttered things into the phone and hung up. "I've got to go, kids. Can we continue this later, Doc?"

"There's not much more to say, I imagine. I was about to leave anyway."

Maggie practically hurled him out of the room. "I'm going to ask Doc about Snuffy. He might be able to do something about it."

Marra said, "Maybe he could, at that. Stick around, Doc. Use the office. So long."

Maggie sat down in the desk chair and I asked, "What's with this Snuffy?"

"It's just one of those things that gets under your skin, Doc, and I can't get it off my mind. Snuffy was the dishwasher at the club. Hell of a sweet little character—a withered-up old guy who'd had it a lot better somewhere along the line. He'd been places and seen things. We used to talk with him between shows. He'd give us everything from philosophy, to tips on the races. We all loved the little man, Doc."

"What happened to him?"

"That's the point. He just disappeared—just didn't come back to work a couple of weeks ago. I wouldn't have thought so much about it, but he was sick when he left—awful sick. I'm afraid he's laid up in some rotten hole someplace, with pneumonia. The last night he worked, his face was puffy and flushed and he finally admitted he didn't feel so good so I took his temperature. I keep a thermometer around on account of the girls. It was more than a hundred and two."

"What was his last name?"

"Nobody knows. Just Snuffy."

"But that's impossible. He worked for the club so he's got to have a Social Security number and a name."

"No. I tried that. He didn't work on the regular pay roll. Phil Lauziere used to chuck him a few dollars every once in a while. A lot of drifting dishwashers work that way."

"You think that Lauziere might have known him? Somewhere else, maybe?" I couldn't see where it would fit anyplace, but it might.

Maggie thought a moment. "I don't think so, Doc. Lauziere had almost nothing to do with Snuffy—hardly spoke to him when he paid him. Come to think of it, Phil raised so much hell about the little fella's giving horse tips to the girls that we used to give Snuffy jiggers so he'd have time to hide his *Racing Form.*"

"Did Snuffy know a lot about racing?"

"He must have. He didn't talk much about himself, but he told us about races he'd seen way back when he was a young fellow—Man o' War and Exterminator and horses like that. He used to tell the kids, 'If you gotta play the races, you better figger out a horse that's got some kind of a chance to win.'" Maggie stared out the dirty window. "Poor little guy!"

"I don't see how I can do much, Maggie—maybe ask around. Some old-timer might remember a horseman called Snuffy. I can try."

"I suppose tramps like that aren't worth a lot of trouble, Doc, but when I think about how rotten they treated him and how, he probably didn't have anybody to give him a hand except us, I can't help feeling awful about it." The spectacle of this big, fair Diana about to burst into tears was a little awe-inspiring. I hurriedly did what I could about it—a pat on the shoulder and a lot of quick words which I began to regret almost immediately.

"Look, Maggie, don't let it get to you. People in show business are the worst suckers in the world for a guy that's run out of luck. This Snuffy is probably in a county hospital someplace getting well. Don't you worry, I'll find him—"

"But how, Doc? Snuffy! . . . You can't find a man with no other name than Snuffy in a city like New York."

"You'd be surprised. The social agencies . . . hospital records . . . police records . . . it shouldn't be too hard. We know within a couple of days of when they handled his case. He'd have to give the name of his most recent employer on any of them."

Maggie cheered up at once. "He would, wouldn't he! You could trace him if he'd been sick enough to call in help."

"Of course! I'll even get my friend, Lieutenant Eddie Marsh, on it. He's the best cop in the business. Now give me as detailed description as you can of this man . . ."

I wrote it all down. There was pitifully little—mostly patched blue shirts, khaki pants, and an old brown overcoat with an undersized and faded old man inside, small, broken shoes, soggy with the greasy drippings of the sink. Maggie guessed his size and weight in the terms of her trade—"Sort of pony-size, Doc. I don't know much about men's weight, but I'd guess him at, maybe, a hundred and ten or fifteen."

When I left Maggie in Fifty-third Street, I had a couple of things to think about—a couple of new things. The fact that Snuffy had found warmth and a few bucks in the steaming kitchen of the Ricky Club didn't seem important. He wouldn't have been the only ex-jock to be found washing dishes for a handout. But the thing that did seem important was something Maggie had said to me just before she hurried off to her dry cleaning. I'd asked her if she could remember anything that the little man had said which could have any bearing on the activities of the people around the club—people he wasn't supposed to know. Maggie had thought it over, there in the street.

"He could have said such things, Doc, without my noticing them too much. Snuffy used to get—oh, philosophical—but he never mentioned any names."

"What sort of things did he say when he got philosophical?"

"There was one thing he said often—any time the girls would gossip about something that went on in the club. He'd say, 'When you get to be as old as I am, and seen the things I've seen, you learn to keep your mouth shut.'"

"Remember the kind of gossip that would bring out a remark like that?"

Maggie had suddenly become excited. "Hey! You know? There was one night three weeks or so ago—it was colder than hell and the dressing rooms were freezing. Between shows, the girls were all hanging around the kitchen end, trying to keep warm. Between batches of dishes, Snuffy was reading the *Racing Form.* Somebody had a bottle of whisky and all of us had a couple of swigs—including Snuffy, Naturally, we were keeping a pretty sharp lookout for the bosses. We'd been out there about ten minutes when one of the girls hollered 'Jiggers!' We hid the bottle and Snuffy stuffed the *Racing Form* back of the drainpipe under the sink just as Rick Fogan barged into the kitchen. His face was almost dead white and he was furious—out of control. He just stood there for a second and then he practically roared, *'Where's Lauziere?'* He scared everybody so much that nobody answered. Then he wheeled around and banged out of the place."

"And where *was* Lauziere?"

"Nobody seemed to know. The girls started to get back to the dressing rooms and one of them, Eve Tillory, said—to nobody in particular—'What goes on in this joint anyway?' Well, Snuffy looked up from his sink with his eyes—I don't know—burning like with some awful fury, I suppose that was the night I began to think he was a little off his rocker, poor fella. He looked straight at Eve and said, 'When you get as old as I am, you learn not to ask questions like that. It ain't always healthy to know the answers.'"

"That was all?"

"That was all, Doc. He just went back to washing his dishes."

"Maybe he was off his rocker, Maggie, but, if my guess is any good, that crack made wonderful sense."

"It wasn't only that. A little later, that night, one of the girls who follows the horses borrowed Snuffy's *Form* from under the sink while he was in back having a smoke—and do you know what?"

"What?"

"The little guy had spent all evening studying a racing paper that was more than a year old!"

5

When I got back to the apartment Mrs. Parter was winding up her operations and everything was back in the precise, scrubbed way she leaves whatever she touches. As she was getting her coat on and I was digging into my wallet she said:

"There's a man waitin' for you in the reception room of the office. I put him in there while I finished up in front. Name's Bradford."

I stuck my head through the office door and called Tom. He came in looking pretty dejected. We shook hands. He smelled of horse.

"I thought I'd come over right after I got through work, Doc." Bradford sat down on the couch and dawdled with his broken-down felt hat. I took it from him and stuck it on the mantel.

"Anything special, Tom?"

In the absence of his hat, he dawdled with an equally broken-down pack of cigarettes. He straightened one out and lit it before he said anything. "Yeah. Very special. I made a hell of a mistake."

"How?"

"I should have rolled up that shank yesterday morning and hung it on the stall door with the halter. Then I should have shut my big yap and kept it shut."

"Can you tell me why? You felt pretty strongly about it when I saw you."

Bradford waited until Mrs. Parter had stuck her head in from the kitchen and said good-by. "Sure I felt strongly about it—so strongly that I forgot a lot of things that are a damned sight more important."

"Such as what, Tom?"

"Such as the effect one cruel, rotten trick like this can have on the lives of a lot of people who didn't have anything to do with it."

I decided to let that alone for a moment, feeling that Tom wouldn't be listing any names. "I was out at the club last night for dinner."

"I know." He didn't explain how and I didn't ask him. Sometime, probably that morning, someone had told him that I'd been at Fogan's place and, at the same time, made statements which would account for his change of heart.

"Do you know that bunch out there, Tom?"

"I was only at the place once. Fogan invited me. I can't go to night clubs and train horses at the same time." He was obviously being defensive.

"I was wondering if you'd ever known the singer—Rita Ross."

Bull's-eye! Bradford stiffened. "What are you trying to prove, Doc? Why should I know a night-club entertainer named Rita Ross?"

"Possibly because, unless I'm badly mistaken, Tom, her father is on your pay roll out at the race track." I made it as gentle as I could—tried not to sound like the district attorney—but Bradford looked as if I'd hit him with something. He opened his mouth a couple of times without saying anything, then shook his head slowly from side to side and sank back into the couch.

"Can we call this whole thing off, Doc? Can we just forget it ever happened? There's nobody hurt except Fogan—so far—and he's upset as hell because I called you in the first place."

"Then you do know Rita? Rita Asher?"

"Of course I know her. I've known her almost as long as I can remember. We were kids at the track together. Old Pop Asher had a string of runners in those days and he and my old man—Lance Bradford—were cronies. Hell! Rita and I learned to exercise horses the same summer."

"How much have you known about her—say—recently?"

"Not much, Doc. Rita went away someplace to study music and I didn't see her for years. When she turned up in New York we ran around together some. Then my dad died and I had to go down home for a spell to settle things up. When I got back I couldn't locate her and finally got busy with horses of my own and gave it up."

"When did you find out she was working for Fogan?"

"Not until after Fogan started talking about my training some horses for him. After that he brought Rita to the track one morning and introduced her as Miss Ross. I didn't crack and neither did she. Later she called me up and told me a lot of stuff about her career and what it meant to her and all that. I told her I didn't figure it was any of my business what she called herself. Then she asked me if I'd give her dad a job. The old man's getting a little slow and he wasn't finding work too easily. It was as simple as that."

"It's not simple any more, Tom."

"What do you mean?"

"I mean just what I say. It's not simple any more. Do you know anything about Rita's present—status—at the Ricky Club?"

"I've taken it for granted that she was Fogan's girl—in some way—if that's what you mean." Tom wasn't finding it easy going.

"What do you mean—'in some way'?"

"Hell, I don't know, Doc." He crushed the light from his cigarette with his thumb and forefinger before he thought of the ash tray. You get pretty careful about cigarettes around a barn. "When I knew Rita she didn't seem like the kind of woman to—sell out for a job."

"From what I'm told, she didn't sell out for a job—at least not to Rick Fogan."

"I don't understand."

"You know Lauziere—Fogan's headwaiter?"

"No. I guess I saw him when I was there. Guy named Phil?"

"That's right—he calls it Philippe."

"I never saw him before. What about him?" Bradford accented the "him."

"Lauziere's the one who got Rita her break—found her singing on some local station."

"So what's that make?"

"Nothing, I guess. He's supposed to have paid for her coaching and to be taking a cut out of her salary."

Tom pulled a Jamaica condition book out of his coat pocket, looked at it blankly, and put it back. "It's all news to me, Doc. I can't see what the hell it has to do with somebody destroying a fine race mare in my barn."

"I can't either, Tom. Maybe it hasn't anything to do with it at all. Maybe it has." I wanted to think about it and couldn't find anything to say. I walked over to the window and looked down into Forty-eighth. Bradford went out into the kitchen and got a glass of water without speaking.

No coincidences anywhere. Rita Asher knew and liked horses. Fogan had owned a string some years before. Rita persuaded Fogan to get back in the game and, quite naturally, recommended Tom Bradford as a reliable trainer. Strong, wrong situations at the Ricky Club. At the barn, such possibilities as Bradford's jealousy, old Pop Asher's probable knowledge of his daughter's situation.

I could hardly blame any of them for wanting to call the whole thing off. Even without the impact of a serious crime, the story would give the newspapers a field day. A night-club owner's race mare murdered in her stall . . . father of Rick Fogan's alleged mistress discovered in employ of trainer . . . lived in poverty while daughter shared fleshpots with former New Orleans gambler! Season that dish with a sinister Lauziere, robbed by Fogan through the years, and you've got quite a yarn.

I came back and sat down across from Bradford. "Look, Tom, did Pop Asher know anything about Rita's—life?"

"Hell, I don't know, Doc. I don't know anything about any of it." The trainer slapped his battered hat on his head. A couple of oat kernels fell to the couch. "Pop quit this morning."

"Why?"

"He didn't say anything. He just came around and did his work—then called for his time. When I asked him why he was leaving he said it was for reasons of his own."

"You didn't follow that up?"

"With a man like old Pop, you don't. We're a funny breed, horsemen—independent as people ever get." Tom got up to go. "Listen, fella, if somebody wanted to hurt Fogan, he's done it. If he wanted to hurt the rest of us, all we've got to do is to chase this thing a little further and we'll make him happy. I don't know what's behind it any more than you do. But I'll tell you one thing. Whatever it is, it isn't going to be pretty and it's going to be awful rough on everybody concerned. Can we forget it, Doc?"

I felt sorry for the guy. "Sure, Tom, we can forget it. I'm damned if I like people who run around killing horses out of spite, but I'm certainly not going to let that get you—or Fogan or anybody else—in trouble."

Bradford stuck out his hand and I took it. "Thanks, Doc. I'll be relieved as hell." He'd started for the door when I remembered Maggie Marra's dishwasher.

"By the way. Did you ever know anybody around the race track called Snuffy?"

"Snuffy?"

"That's it."

After a while he said, "I don't remember anybody at all by that name, Doc." He thanked me again and rattled down in the elevator. I stood in the doorway for a moment, conscious of the things he had left behind him—a very pronounced odor of horse and the distinct impression that somebody was really putting the pressure on him.

6

I had piously intended to mind my own business after my talk with Tom, but when I went up to Tello's for a sandwich after I got through with patients the next day I ran into Joe Herrick. He was sitting alone in a booth. The place was packed and I was looking around for a table when he spoke.

"Hello, Doc." He displayed a tremendous lot of bargain dentistry. "Sit down."

I sat down. "Thanks. This used to be a nice quiet place."

"Not no more, it ain't. Not since Papa Tello turned it over to the kid." The waiter came and took the orders. "I seen you at the Ricky Club the other night."

"Yeah?"

"Yeah. You sure get around."

"Get around? I don't go to clubs much. That was an occasion. Rick Fogan invited us out."

"He sure got a bad break—Fogan—losing that nice filly like that." My skin prickled a little. Herrick was telegraphing his punches, but he was throwing them. I said:

"Yes. It was a damned shame. He told me about it that night."

"Oh? *He* told *you* about it that night?"

"Yes." Herrick gave me a crooked grin before he went back to designing his napkin with his fork. I got sore. "Anything wrong with that?"

"Wrong? No. I was the guy that was wrong. You know, Doc, I could've swore *you* was telling *him* about it."

"Why would you think that, Joe?"

"Well, bein' as you were out to his barn that morning and all that, I kinda took it for granted. You know how it is."

"You get around some yourself, don't you!" Anybody could have seen me at the track. This guy, I had to figure, was poking around for something else, and I wanted to know it as badly as he did. "Are you trying to ask questions, Joe? Or is this just lunch conversation?"

"Just lunch conversation, Doc, and here it comes. You shoulda ordered them ham hocks and beans."

I shoulda, at that. I forgot to tell the waiter I like my ham-and-cheese-on-whole-wheat dry. They had slopped it up with broken-down tomatoes and patent mayonnaise. For a while we ate in such silence as Joe's chomping tactics would permit, then, timing it carefully so that he'd have a jowlful of ham hocks, I asked:

"Ever hear of a guy around the track called Snuffy, Joe?"

His inability to say anything was not conditioned entirely by the fact that he had a mouthful. He was pretty well startled. That he knew something about Snuffy was certain. If he knew it, Patsy Dahl would know it better—Patsy Dahl, who had hurried into Fogan's office when he got to the club the other night! I let Herrick finish his mouthful in peace. He finally got around to his stall.

"Snuffy—Snuffy—I can't remember no one like that around the track, Doc."

"Okey. I just wondered." Casual . . .

"Anything special?" He was frightened—but he was as interested as hell. I thought I'd give him a little something beside ham hocks to chew on.

"Oh no. A friend just asked me to give him a message if I saw him."

"Didn't your friend know this guy's right name? Only Snuffy?"

"I don't know. Perhaps he did. I didn't pay much attention to the whole thing. I don't suppose it amounted to much. He just said 'If you happen to see a little guy called Snuffy at the track' . . . you know how those things are."

He fooled around with this awhile and then came up with an inspiration. "You know, Doc? I'm seein' a fella tonight that might just happen to know this Snuffy you're talkin' about. I could give him the message." I tried to look doubtful. "That is, if it would be any help to you . . ."

I hauled a buck out of my pocket and left it, with some regret, for the sodden mass I'd eaten. "Don't bother, Joe, thanks. The message was—well, you know—sort of confidential."

When I got back to the apartment I called Eddie Marsh at headquarters. It seems silly, but I never get over being a little awed by the big cop at work, though he ranks next to Katie in my affections.

"Marsh!" That's what I mean. He hollers it.

"This is Doc, Eddie. You sound awfully busy . . ."

"How do you want me to sound? You're a taxpayer, aren't you? I'll do birdcalls if you demand it. What you got on your mind?"

"I'm trying to locate a guy named Snuffy who might have been taken to one of the hospitals in the last week or so—or maybe he's just lying sick someplace and needs to be taken to one."

"What's the rest of his name?"

"I haven't the slightest idea."

Eddie started hollering again. "Goddammit, Doc, why don't you ever make sense? Have you got a good description of the guy?"

"Not complete—but he was jockey-size, over fifty, gray hair, worked as a dishwasher at—"

"Where does he live? Where did he live last?"

"I don't know. He was just a little guy that came along and got a job dishwashing at Rick Fogan's club and he—"

This sort of thing went on for quite a while and I finally ended up by having Maggie Marra phone Marsh as complete a description as she could dig up. As the calls back and forth progressed, Eddie got more and more irked at my unloading such a mess of menial police work on his Homicide Bureau in the name of friendship. It finally turned out that he'd worked all night and had a date to go bowling before he went home to bed.

In the late afternoon I decided to do some prowling in the neighborhood of the Ricky Club. It seemed a fair possibility that Snuffy had gone out to get sandwiches for the girls or a beer for himself and might have left something specific behind. Starting from the stage door of the building, I looked around. There was a liquor store near the corner.

"The little fella from the club? Yeah. He come in here once in a while for a pint. No. I never knew his name or nothin' about him."

I tried the delicatessen. Yes. He'd been in for beer in bottles—usually a dozen or more. Nothing else. Around the corner there was a good-sized saloon. They didn't know him. I turned back and went west a block. On that corner was a dingy little place down three or four steps from the street. I tried that. The bartender was reading the comics—or whatever it is people do who sit and stare at them. I ordered an Old Forester and water. He hunted for the bottle and found it without conversation. A cat came out from somewhere in the back and kept looking at me. If I'd been an obstetrician I'd have thought she meant something by it. Finally the bartender folded up the comics and just sat. I broke the ice.

"Tell me. Did a little pint-size fellow named Snuffy used to come in here? He was a dishwasher at the Ricky Club."

"Well, I'll tell you, Mac. I ain't been here very long and don't know a lot of the people around the neighborhood. Maybe you better come in tomorrow morning and talk to the boss. He opens up."

"I see." Another blank.

"You with the cops?"

"No. I'm a doctor." I ordered another Forester and wondered if the fact I wasn't with the cops would help any. He poured the whisky and water without speaking. A man and woman came in and sat in one of the booths. The bartender took their order and filled it. When he had settled down again he said:

"Come to think of it, there might have been a man that could have been called Snuffy come in here a few times. He owe you some money?"

"Hell, no! The little guy was sick for a day or two and then disappeared. The girls at the club were worried about him and asked me to try to locate him. We're afraid he may have pneumonia someplace and nobody to help him."

He swabbed the bar absently. "You got a card with you, Doc?"

I showed him some identification. I didn't have a card. My couple of years of sabbatical leave are petering out fast enough without my scattering cards around town. He put on a pair of battered glasses and looked the stuff over. "James C. Connor, eh?"

"That's right."

"That would be Doc Connor—I mean *the* Doc Connor?"

"The only James Cardigan Connor, if that's what you mean."

The man looked at me over his spectacles. "The Doc Connor I'm talking about works with the cops."

"The man you're talking about worked *twice* with his best friend—who happens to be on the cops. In both cases somebody very nasty and very wrong was involved. Is this Snuffy very nasty —and very wrong?"

"Okey, Doc. I heard a lot of other things about you, too, besides you helped the cops. The last time I seen Snuffy the only thing he was was very sick."

"When was this?"

He wiped the bar some more and stared at the rag. "I think maybe it was like two weeks ago. Ten days. He used to come in around six o'clock in the evening—before he went to work. He'd have a few beers with me. Said they charge the help full price at the club."

The people in the booth hollered "Chris!" and asked for refills. Chris went over and took care of them. It was getting dark out—almost too dark to see the feet walking on the sidewalk through the window above. The bartender came back and poured me a drink on the house without asking me. He stood there and watched me mix it.

"So you think Snuffy may be sick in his room and nobody to help him, Doc?"

"That's what the girls in the show are worrying about. Look, Chris, did Snuffy ever tell you what his last name was—or where he lived?"

"He never told me his name or where he lived or anything about himself except the last time he was here. He said he might be in some kind of trouble."

"Did he say what the trouble might have been?"

"No. He said . . . the guy was full of fever and kind of dopey . . . he said he'd planned to get out of town but he felt too sick to go. He thought it had something to do with his catarrh. His head was always stuffed up. That's probably why they called him Snuffy."

"But he never told you where he lived?"

"No. But I found out."

Jackpot! "Oh? How?"

"It was a rough night out and I sent him home in a cab. Nick Latale stands a hack on the corner and I called him. I asked Nick where he took the fella and he told me some dirty-looking basement room uptown. I wrote it down—just in case."

It was trying to snow—wet and unpleasant—when I climbed into the cab at the corner.

"Where to, Mac?" The driver put down his pulp-paper magazine which he'd been reading by the dashlight.

"Fourteen-ten and a half Harker, Nick."

Nick turned on his meter and card lights and twisted around to peer at me. "You ain't supposed to call me Nick until I turn my lights on. Then everybody does."

"Chris told me you'd probably be on the corner. I'm trying to locate the little guy you took home to Harker Street a couple of weeks ago."

"City dick, maybe, eh?"

"Doctor."

"The little guy sure needed one when I seen him last."

"I hope he still needs one."

We drove on without further conversation. The wet snow on the windshield and the slippery streets kept Nick at his job. I decided to drop off at the corner of Harker and nose around. There was a shabby cigar store and a delicatessen at the intersection. The lights of a neighborhood saloon glared out from down the block.

Harker Street was strictly tenements—four-story brick, mostly, and in terrible repair. Fourteen-ten seemed more disreputable, if possible, than the rest. Fourteen-ten and a half, I found, was indicated by a crudely lettered sign pointing down the areaway toward the rear of the building. I could see only one light burning in the whole place—a couple of yellowed windows on the second-floor front.

I turned down the areaway and walked back past trash cans and rubbish. Three quarters of the way back I found a railing, two or three steps down, and a door. There was no light. I tried the door. It was not only unlocked but ajar. For some reason that I have yet to figure out, I was pleased to find the door open. Maybe it was because I wouldn't have to do any housebreaking. Also, maybe it was because I'm not too smart.

Rats or something made a small sound as I entered the hallway that apparently led off to the furnace room of the building. I could smell coal burning and the passage was warm. I closed the door behind me and got out my little pen-sized flashlight. There was another door on my left. I opened it and listened before I went into the room. Then I used my light again to find the bulb hanging from the ceiling.

The place was a storeroom—trunks and boxes piled in one end. In the other, a bed, an old morris chair, and a table. An apple box with a piece of faded chintz tacked around it stood beside the bed. On it were neatly stacked a lot of racing papers. They were all from the early months of the previous year—February, March, April. I picked one at random and looked in the alphabetical list of entries. There it was! Armada! She was entered in a race for maiden two-year-olds in the South. I looked for the next day's *Form* and found it—in direct order of date. I left my flashlight on the apple box and moved under the light to read the chart.

The light went out.

I stood frozen to the paper in my hands and waited. I heard two or three soft steps in back of me and then found out what I'd been waiting for.

"All right, nosy, go out the way you came and keep going."

I restrained two distinct impulses. What did Doc Wheeler used to call it? Fight or flight. Neither seemed practical at the moment, so I just stood there.

"Shake the lead, burglar. What do you want? Trouble?"

Then he put the light on me—a shock of flashlight that hit me full in the face. I closed my eyes and turned my head. He put the light on the door.

"There it is. I'll follow you. Get going!"

I had no choice but to go out the door and down the passage. The man walked behind with the flashlight, always keeping his distance. At one time I thought he had come closer. Footsteps. But the light didn't come any closer. Just the footsteps. As I came to the outside door I stopped to open it. Then we all stopped. Then everything stopped.

I remember grabbing at a coat sleeve as I fell. Camel's hair. Camel's hair—and heavy.

7

A woman's voice was droning and I opened my eyes to see a huge, weather-beaten mug staring at me. Blue-black jaws told me that the woman's voice had to be coming from someplace else. I gave it up and closed my eyes again. The voice went on . . .

". . . then, right in, the middle of the program, all the lights went off and my radio quit. Solly, that's my boy here, come down to fix the fuse and stumbled over this man . . ."

On and on it went. ". . . would you believe it, Officer? The switch was off." A Henry Aldrich added, "Yeah! Somebody musta threw the switch. Maybe this guy."

Someplace in the distance a siren was howling, coming toward us. The big face near mine said, "He didn't hit himself over the head, that's sure." The cop dug around in my hair. "If that welt wasn't made by a blackjack, I should be on the Fire Department."

Rubber squealed around the corner and the siren growled itself out. A white coat appeared next to the big face. A slightly more mature Henry Aldrich said, "What's the matter with this guy?"

As distinctly as I could, I said, "I think you'll find it's a traumatic encephalopathy."

The young man said, "Good God!"

Having proved what an ass I can make of myself—even in the most trying circumstances—I drifted off again. Impressions jumbled themselves together and I didn't attempt to separate them. The siren whooped. The stretcher bounced. "Put his head sideways . . . a little more this way." The X ray buzzed. The pillow felt swell. Then the ice pack felt cold as hell. I must have slept.

Some time later I squinted an eye open to observe a newspaper, an expanse of blue serge, and the largest pair of feet I have ever seen on a human being of normal stature. Under any other conditions I would have known those feet anywhere. As it was, I said:

"Who are you?"

The paper came down and Eddie Marsh said, "Who the hell do you think? Do you know anybody else that would give up his evening to sit by your bed of pain?"

"What time is it?"

"A quarter to ten. How do you feel?"

"Terrible."

"You haven't got any fractures or anything." Eddie put the paper away and came over to stand by the bed. "What's with this housebreaking?"

"I was looking for a guy."

"Snuffy?"

"Yes. I found out where he lives."

"Lived."

"What do you mean?"

"He's dead. I got it all for you." Marsh pulled up the small chair and hauled out his notebook. "You never listen to me, do you! I could have saved you that sore head if you had. I wasn't perfectly sure until they told me you'd got sapped at the same address. The people from that house called a neighborhood doctor named Bardon who's done some charity work around there. It seems that a Patrick W. Goddard who had a room in the back basement was seriously ill. Day after that the man died and his body was turned over to the authorities for burial. He had told the doctor he had no living relatives—and no money."

"So that was Snuffy!"

"Apparently. The Missing Persons Bureau invariably checks the morgue and, from Mrs. Marra's description, we arrived at Goddard." Eddie hauled out a pack of cigarettes. "Smoke bother you?"

"Lord, no! Give me one, will you?" He gave me a cigarette and held his lighter. He sat down again and stretched his legs under the bed.

"Who do you think hit you, Doc?"

"I wouldn't have any idea." It could have been any one of a lot of people. "Eddie, did you, by any chance, look around the room where this man lived—at the place I got knocked out, I mean?"

"No. I don't go out on stuff like that. One of the men on the desk recognized your name and called me. Why?"

"I want to know if the police found a stack of old *Racing Forms* in the room—beside the bed. Probably one on the floor.

Eddie laughed so loud one of the nurses poked her head in the door. "Horses again, Doc? You can get into more trouble over horses than most guys can over women. What would you want a lot of old *Racing Forms* for?"

"I haven't the foggiest notion. That is, I haven't any idea why *I'd* want them. But if they're gone I'll know that somebody else wanted them badly enough to get awfully tough about it."

"Maybe you'd better tell me some more."

"First, have you any way of finding out if those papers were left in the room?"

"If the radio car men who went in looked the room over, there's a pretty good chance they'd have noticed. I can call in and see." He picked up the phone by the bed—the hospital had rolled out the rug when they found out I was a physician. Eddie rambled on in headquarters jargon, waited for an answer, gave the number of my room, and hung up. "They'll call me back. The car's still out so we're sure to reach them. Now tell me about it."

"Take off your badge?"

The big cop gave me a quick take. "Look here, Doc, you've damned near had that badge off me for good a couple of times. If it's police business . . ."

"It isn't."

"Breaking into people's cellars and getting sapped over the head is police business. You're lucky there are some people downtown who trust you."

"Dammit, I went on a mission of mercy. The door was open and—"

"I know, I know. Don't defend yourself to me. Just tell me what goes." Eddie jammed around and found me an ash tray. "You don't have to be so coy about it—you know what's police business and what isn't."

"Sure I know, Eddie. I'm sort of stuck with a story that concerns a lot of other people's business."

"Is that something new?"

"Well, it's one of those things that would embarrass some people. If it were a police matter it would really be a mess."

"But it isn't, you say."

"No. Not unless somebody sees fit to make a complaint. It's a case of malicious mischief—I think that's what you call it."

"What sort of malicious mischief?"

"Maybe you call it wanton destruction of property. As a matter of fact, it was equicide."

"You mean somebody killed somebody's horse?"

"That's right. A race horse. A good one."

"What a lousy trick! So you've appointed yourself the Equicide Squad." Eddie, somehow, just didn't laugh about it. He's a nice cop.

"More or less, yes. I thought you might help me."

"Noons, nights, and Sundays?"

"Not so much with your time, but with things like you did about Snuffy. I've run into something that involves right people and wrong people in the same mess. So far I can't tell them apart. Will you listen and keep it to yourself?"

Eddie put the little chair aside and dragged the big one over to the bed. When he'd settled down he said, "Every mess is that way. Give."

I told him the story in as much detail as I could. He stopped me at point after point with clarifying questions—wrote stuff in the back of his notebook.

"You say the halter, and the whaddyacallit—the shank were left on the ground? Like the guy was interrupted?"

"Yes. Interrupted or simply wanted Fogan to know that he'd been there."

"No. I won't buy that." Eddie seldom expressed opinions which weren't drawn directly from evidence. "The sort of a heel that would kill a man's horse would have found some snide way of letting him know directly—not of letting *everybody* know. I think he was about to be surprised by the watchman or somebody."

The phone rang. Eddie picked it up and said, "Marsh." A loose receiver diaphragm rasped with the heavy voice on the other end. Eddie held the instrument away from his ear so I could hear.

". . . Robinson—a good man. He checked the premises thoroughly. The woman who runs the place said they hadn't gotten around to cleaning it since Goddard was taken away, but that she had looked in yesterday to get something out of a trunk and nothing had been disturbed. When Robinson and Schultz went in, the mattress was on the floor and ripped open on both sides. There were no *Racing Forms*—or old papers of any kind. That cover it, Lieutenant?"

"Yeah. Thanks, Willis. Anything reported stolen?"

"Nothing."

"How was the entry effected?"

"There's no evidence of forcing. The woman can't find her key today and thinks maybe she left it in the door. Outside of what Doc Connor ran into, it looks like a routine prowl job."

"That's the way it looks, all right. Some people where Goddard worked told Doc he was sick and Doc went out to see him. He must've run into the prowlers." Eddie grinned at me. "Who you got on it now?"

"Young Benning. Know him?"

"New broom! He'll turn the place inside out. Okey, thanks, Willis."

Marsh hung up and sat down again in the big chair. "Where was the mattress when you saw it?"

"On the bed—with a dirty quilt over it. The quilt was sort of piled on. I could see the mattress. It hadn't been cut."

"Well, your pals—I'm sure there were two of them or you wouldn't have had that illusion about the flashlight in back of you—your pals sapped you over the head, one of them probably watched you, and the other went back and worked the room over. Then they beat it with the racing papers. It wouldn't have taken long. By the time the old lady and the boy had located a light and groped their way down to the fuse box, they could have cleaned up and gone." Eddie lit us a couple more cigarettes. "Now tell me the rest of it."

I finished up the story, leaving out nothing—Lauziere, Rita Asher, Maggie Marra's statements, Bradford's visit—everything.

When I'd finished, he lay back in his chair and looked at me, smiling. "You know, Doc? I could read that in the *Saturday Evening Post* and I'd know you had something to do with it. When you get yourself involved in a situation you don't kid around." He got up and stretched. "I'm off. They'll let you out of here in the morning if you don't get any dizzy spells or what not." He put on his hat and headed for the door. "Better call Katie when I go. She's waiting for it."

"Good Lord! Why? How would she know I was here?"

"I thought I'd better tell her before the bulldog editions of the morning papers come out."

"I hadn't thought of that." I had a bad moment wondering what the news story might start. "Eddie! What have they got? The papers?"

"Just what I gave 'em, pal." The big guy leaned against the door and leered at me. "It ought to build up that charity practice of yours some. Should make a first-class yarn—young sporting physician, noted among the big and small alike of Broadway for his great heart, bludgeoned by robbers while searching for stricken bum."

"Quiet—before I throw up. Did you name the bum?"

"Definitely not. When I heard the address I clammed up on Snuffy—for no particular reason except that I suspected you were involved in some unpleasant way with him. Good night."

I listened to his big, flat feet pounding down the linoleum for a moment before I laughed. Then my head hurt and I called Katie.

"Jimmy darling! Tell me how you are. I've been terribly worried. Eddie called and—"

"I'm perfectly all right. Stop acting so broken down about it. Eddie Marsh had no right to worry you." I couldn't, somehow, accept her sympathy when the damned thing had happened because I never can mind my own business. "As a matter of fact, the whole thing was—"

"I know all about it. Eddie told me the story. As you know perfectly well, I've never liked your taste in patients nor the places they live, but when you brave a tough section at night looking for a poor—"

"Will you shut up and listen. I'm all right. I've got a bump on my head and I'll be out of here in the morning. I'll call you."

"Out of where? Eddie just said you'd call."

Where? It hadn't occurred to me to ask. "Why . . ." I had to look at the telephone number. "Why, Knickerbocker Hospital. I seem to be there."

Katie's voice was deeply disturbed. "Then you must have been—unconscious when they brought you in! Oh, Jimmy! Do you suppose they would let me in if I came over? Like relations and all that?"

"Of course they wouldn't let you in, sweet. There'd be a scandal. Besides, I've got an icecap on my head and I look funny. You just forget it. I'll see you tomorrow."

". . . and tomorrow and tomorrow and tomorrow . . ." It isn't often that the gallant Katie goes starry-eyed—never, certainly, when I'm around and healthy. I clutched the phone. "Oh, Jimmy . . ."

"You *do* love me, don't you, darling?"

"Of course I do. Of course!"

"Will you marry me?"

"Certainly not. But I'll damned well hang around to see that people don't slug you over the head while you're trying to render a fine, human service."

"I—"

"I'm so terribly proud of you, Doc dear! I don't care if you never treat another—er—clean patient as long as you live! Just keep on doing as you are, will you, darling?"

"I'm afraid so . . ."

"Good night, then. Call me in the morning, will you?"

"Of course I will. Good night."

All of which goes to show, I suppose, that I can be an ass, also, under less trying conditions.

8

When I got back to the apartment in the morning the place looked like the floor of the Stock Exchange. The janitor, in despair, had opened the waiting room, which was swarming with practically all the local characters I had ever treated—plus two reporters. I barricaded myself in my office and nursed my aching head. Finally I gave up sulking and went to the door and addressed the multitude: "Look, folks. All of you couldn't have got worse at once. We've got about twice as many patients as usual this morning." There were quite a few good-natured grins around. "Also, I see a couple of very healthy-looking newspapermen here."

One of them said, "Look, Doc! We wanta—"

"I think we can save a lot of office time if I get this over with right now. Out here. I'll tell you all about it. Then, if you're really in need of treatment, stick around and get it as usual. If you aren't, beat it. That goes for the reporters too."

"But listen, Doc, there's a hell of a story in it if you tie it up to the Peters case and—"

Big Dave Zwick, a bull of a man whom I've been treating for, of all things, anemia, stood up directly in front of the reporters. "Do you want I should throw these punks out, Doc?"

A general mutter of approval ran around the room and the reporter shut up. "Not yet, Dave. Save it." My head was banging so hard I wouldn't have cared if he'd thrown them all out. "Here's what happened. A friend told me where a man might be alone and very ill—asked me to try to help him. I went to the place, found the door unlocked, walked in, and got hit over the head by some prowlers. They had evidently thought the man was a miser or something because they had searched his room and ripped open the mattress. I didn't see anybody because they turned a flashlight in my face. I spent the night as a guest of the city in the Knickerbocker Hospital and I feel like the devil this morning. Now, next time I look out here I want to see about half as many of you as there were before:—and no reporters."

I went back into the office and pushed the buzzer for the first patient. By the time I'd pushed it for the last time I was pretty well pooped and went into the apartment. It was one o'clock. I lay down on the couch and wondered who, among the people I had met through Rick Fogan, wanted something a dishwasher named Snuffy Goddard could have hidden in that rat's nest of his.

I guess I went to sleep. The downstairs buzzer woke me and I staggered over and pushed the button. Then I went to the bathroom and splashed some cold water on my face and tenderly brushed my hair a little. My whole scalp hurt. Somebody knocked at the door. It was Rita. Looking very . . . very.

"How do you do, Doctor? I hope you got my note."

"Note? I'm afraid not. But come in, won't you?" She walked past me, trailing an afterscent of lavender. I gave the odor a mental double-take and surveyed the retreating costume. Very tasty. A soft-lined dark suit and a small hat with a vestigial veil. It was all very Yardley and early afternoonish—and should never have appeared west of Fifth Avenue. I started revising my ideas.

"I'm so sorry about the note, Doctor." She sat down and made quick business with a very clean pair of white gloves. "Do you, by any chance, ever look at your mail?"

"The mail. Oh yes—that is, quite often." I went over and picked up a pile of stuff from the desk. Among the drug-house announcements was a letter addressed in a bold vertical hand. The corner card said Rita Ross. "Forgive me, Miss Ross, I apparently—"

"Never mind reading it now. I simply asked if you'd be at home this afternoon. You are. So, unless you have something to do, I'd like to talk to you."

"Of course." I sat across from her. She stared steadily at something over my head. I realized, finally, that she was checking up on my bump.

"You seem to be getting a black eye." Almost casual. Just the right amount of neighborly interest. It was news to me.

"Good Lord! Am I?"

"Your right one. It's purplish."

"I was playing games last night and somebody loosened up a piece of my scalp. Sometimes you get a black eye from that sort of thing—blood seeping around underneath."

"I read about it in the papers this morning." Rita made a gesture toward her bag and I gave her a cigarette. "I understand that the man you were looking for had been a dishwasher at the club."

"That's right. Maggie Marra told me about him."

"I remember seeing him." She studied some horse pictures on the wall above the fireplace. "However, that's not what I came to talk about. It's something else." She laughed a little—uneasily. "It may be difficult . . ."

"I take it for granted you didn't drop in for tea—although that would be very pleasant. By and large, Rita, most people think their problems are worse than anybody else's. A physician gets a good deal of that, you know."

"I keep forgetting you're a doctor . . ."

"So do I—for some reason. But I am, and I've seen a lot of things happen to a lot of people. Most of them come off pretty well when they get around to talking stuff out. May I get you a drink? I have only bourbon whisky."

"Oh. I think so. Yes. Will you, please?"

I banged around in the kitchen awhile to let her settle down. The woman was about to blow a fuse and I wanted her story. I remembered Eddie Marsh saying that, where a lot of people were concerned with a tense situation, the best thing was to wait around until somebody got squirmy and started to tell you things. Maybe this would be it.

Rita accepted the drink gratefully, took a man-size pull at it, and set it down on the end table. I clinked the ice in my glass and waited. She wiped her hands on a small handkerchief and looked up.

"Doctor, what sort of trouble is Rick Fogan in?" Just like that.

I studied my drink and organized my position. "I don't like to answer questions with questions, Rita—but you've started too far into the script. Is Rick in trouble?"

"I'm sure of it."

"Why—how?"

"A lot of things tell me he's in some sort of trouble. Do you, by any chance, know what my right name is?"

"Yes. I know."

"Mind telling me how you know?"

"Katie Storm remembered you."

"I'm glad it was that way. She's a very beautiful girl. I was afraid it might have come to you through my father."

"Pop? Why would he come to me with that?"

"Because he's coming to you with something that's made him furious—I've never seen him so incensed. He stopped at my apartment yesterday afternoon and announced that he'd quit his job."

"Tom Bradford told me."

"Did Tom tell you why?"

"No. He just said Pop asked for his time and wouldn't explain." I had a pretty good hunch, though. The old man had been around horses too long not to recognize trouble when he saw it. "Did he tell you?"

"Not why he quit." Rita went after her drink again. Held her handkerchief around the cold glass. "He said some rather unpleasant things, though. I wouldn't have thought much about them except for the fact that Rick has been acting so strangely lately."

"How lately?"

"The last few days."

"Before he lost the mare?"

"Yes. Before that."

"What did Pop have to say that was so—unpleasant? Will you tell me?"

"Well . . ." She came up with another nervous laugh. "It was mostly about me. Pop is awfully stern in his funny way. He's never liked my being in night-club work. I think he's always wanted me to be a horse trainer."

"Could you?"

She laughed nicely this time. "I certainly could. There isn't much about a race horse that I haven't had some experience with."

"That's what Tom Bradford told me—after I'd found out who you were, of course. Now what did Pop say?"

"He came in and wouldn't even sit down. He acted like one of the prophets out of the Old Testament pronouncing somebody's doom. He said he'd quit his job because he wouldn't work for a bunch of crooks any more—no matter how much he liked Tom. He reminded me that I was of age and it wasn't any of his business if I chose to work for them—but that the whole bunch—including Tom—was going to get into trouble and that I'd better get out."

"Did he explain himself?"

"Pop? Never. He simply delivered his speech and stalked out. Poor old Pop—in his Sunday suit . . ." She ground out her cigarette, groping for the ash tray without looking.

"Have you reason to believe there's anything in what your father said? Is that why you've come to me?"

"I don't know—frankly. What Pop said did disturb me in light of—other things that have happened." She looked at me very directly. "I wondered if your being around the other night meant anything special. After all, you have been connected with some investigations and that sort of thing, haven't you?"

"A couple of times, yes." I decided, at least for the moment, that somebody had sent this young lady on an errand. "Tell me about the other things that have made you—suspicious."

"Not suspicious, Doctor. One has to direct suspicions at someone or other. Apprehensive, perhaps, would cover it better."

"Then what has happened to make you apprehensive?"

Rita finished her drink slowly and settled back. "First, Rick Fogan's behavior. Perhaps you know—or have guessed—that he and Phil Lauziere don't get along."

"I've observed that. They don't go to much trouble to disguise it."

"They used to—even a few weeks ago. Lately it's been very bad. They had a fearful row the night you came to the club—before you got there."

"Over what?"

"Over you, as a matter of fact. At least Rick's orders about where you were to sit and how you were to be treated and all that were what started it. But I don't think that part of it is important. The important thing, to me, is the fact that Rick seems to be in some sort of a spot and Phil Lauziere must know it."

That could make sense. "Oh? And Lauziere is bearing down?"

"Hard. He's practically taking over."

". . . and it isn't like Fogan to stand for it."

"Definitely not. Rick has always handled Phil as a matter of course. The fact that Lauziere hated him has never bothered Fogan in the least. I've spoken to him about it. He simply shrugged it off with some statement to the effect that he wouldn't let personal feelings cost him the best headwaiter in New York." She did a little shrugging herself. "Now Rick has taken to peeking around corners. I think he's afraid of something—or somebody."

"Lauziere, maybe?"

"I don't know. Maybe."

"There are other things, you say?"

"One other. It frightened me and—perhaps more than anything else—gave me the idea the Rick might be in trouble. It happened the night you were at the club. Just before the show I went back to Fogan's office to get my lighter. I couldn't find it in my dressing room and decided I'd left it when we'd had cocktails. Just as I came down the hall a man stepped out of the office. It was Patsy Dahl—a person who represents everything nobody wants around the club. When I went to the door I naturally expected to find Rick there. He wasn't."

"Dahl had been looking around."

"Wouldn't you think so? He wasn't just standing in the door or anything—like he'd poked his head in looking for Rick. He opened the door, came out, and closed it carefully behind him. I saw all that."

"Did you tell Rick?"

"Yes. I told him right away."

"How did he take it?"

"He didn't bat an eye—simply said, 'He was probably looking for me. I'll go over and see what he wants.' I feel sure that, unless there had been some pressure on him, he would have stormed." She smiled. "And now may we please go back to where we started—in the middle of the script?"

"Yes. I haven't the slightest idea of what sort of trouble Fogan may be in—or if he's in any trouble. I do suspect that someone is running around with a hell of a grudge against him and would like to do him dirt. What about Lauziere? What's he like?"

"I've never been able to make him out. He's cross and severe with the help and nobody much likes him—except me."

"But you like him?"

She tilted her head back and there was unnecessary challenge in her eyes. "Why shouldn't I? He pulled me out of a one-horse local radio station and spent his own money to have me coached. Then he had the guts to insist that I be featured in the show. For all Rick Fogan's big gestures, he wouldn't have had either the taste or the courage to take a bet like that!"

This time I did a lot of very fast revising. "Hey! Wait a minute! Is that any way to be talking about the guy? I was of the opinion that—"

She froze. "You were of the opinion that *what,* Doctor?"

Talk about old Pop acting like a prophet of doom! She stood up and picked her gloves off the end table in the same motion. "I got the idea the other night that you and Fogan . . ."

"Unfortunately, a number of people have that idea—including my father. Very possibly their criticism might have been justifiable until the last few weeks." She walked toward the door—rather slowly. I trailed behind. She turned, faced me directly. "It no longer applies. I have never in my life disliked another human being so much as I dislike Rick Fogan."

9

I hadn't put Rita and Lauziere together in my mind before. The dark little man with the smooth manner, the apparent background of horses, and a sullen, brooding hatred of Fogan could be, I thought, the possible answer to all the questions. Fogan had told me that his headwaiter "managed to hear a lot of things" but he had neglected to point out that Rita was in a position to hear a lot more.

One thing didn't fit. Unless Lauziere was an actor as well as a restaurateur, he wasn't the man who'd spoken to me in Snuffy Goddard's basement room. The man who held the light on me had been tough—just plain, natively tough.

My number-one suspect for the flashlight holder came to see me that evening. I had been back half an hour or so from dinner when the apartment buzzer sounded. It was the button in the hall—not the one in the vestibule—but I hadn't heard the elevator. I opened the door and Patsy Dahl stood there wearing a heavy camel's-hair coat.

"Hello, Doc. Got a minute?"

"Sure. Come in."

He walked into the room without taking off his hat. I half expected to see Joe Herrick in the hall but Dahl had come alone. I said, "Sit down, Patsy. Take off your coat and hat. What you got on your mind?"

He sat and dragged off his hat. "I got a coupla things on my mind, Doc. I think maybe it's time you and I had a little talk."

"That's okey with me—but I can't quite figure out what we've got to talk about." If Dahl had come to do the talking, I would listen very carefully.

"You know, pal, I don't believe that." Patsy added a very chummy leer. "I been around town for a while, myself. I don't kid too easy."

I rejected the idea of leering back. Dahl would be used to that. The so-called knowing look is stock in trade with his kind. "If you came to talk about what happened to me last night, Patsy, it's all in the papers."

"I guess I don't read the right papers."

"What do you mean by that?"

"I looked at all of 'em pretty good—including tonight's. All I could find was a lot of hooey about your looking for a charity patient. That I didn't come up to talk about."

"All right. That's fine. So you didn't come up to talk about that. What did you come up to talk about?" I was getting a little sore. Also I was getting a little excited.

"Listen, Doc. If anyone would've ast me who knows the score around this end of town, I would've said Doc Connor. I never knew you in a personal way but I know a lot about you. Everybody does. You can write a better morning line than any horse handicapper in town. You know fights. You get around with the top sporting crowd. You—"

"Goddammit, Dahl, that's *my* business. What the hell has it got to do with you?" The guy was getting to me—on a very touchy subject. He leered again and I nearly jumped him.

"Don't flip your lid, pal. I'll just speak my piece and tell you what business it is of mine—and get out." I fussed with a cigarette and shut up. "The way I figure it, Doc, what's your business and what's mine have got mixed up. As I say, you know the score. But you always kept your nose clean. That's hard to do around this town and still make a dollar. One of the ways you kept your nose clean is by working with the cops."

I started to holler again and held off.

"So, naturally, I figure that if you go prowling around in some bum's basement room and get socked on the head, *if* you're working with the cops, nothing is said, see?"

"I don't—but go on."

"The hell you don't. But if you're not on it with the cops—if you're on some angle of your own—you give the cops some phony story like the one in the papers today. *And,* because they're your pals, sometimes, they buy it. Maybe you see now?"

"What makes you think the story was phony?"

"What are we—kids, Doc—that we gotta play games? I'm clockin' some horses at the track and on the way to the stand I see you at Tom Bradford's barn. In the *Form* that night I read where a horse in Tom's barn has died of heart failure that morning. So far it's okey. Lots of trainers would rather have you than any vet in town. So it's okey up to there."

"And where does it start to be—not okey?"

"Now maybe you're making sense. It starts to get not okey first when I see you with Rick Fogan that night—Fogan and the girl." Dahl took a stick of gum out of his pocket, peeled it carefully, and shoved it into his mouth.

"Why isn't that okey? Can't Rick return a favor by inviting me to dinner?"

"Sure." He spoke softly. "Sure, Doc. He can return a favor by giving you an all-expense honeymoon to Niagara Falls too. But you don't take it, see? Any more than you take a lousy free meal at that trap up there—with a table set for two. This is the first time I knew it was for free. That makes it more so." He looked around the room. "Look, pal. You don't charge people nothing to take care of them, but you do pretty well for yourself. I'm not saying I know how you do it—but you don't do it on free meals at the Ricky Club."

I felt my face get stiff. "So what, Dahl?"

"So maybe I wouldn't have thought much about it except that I was already looking for something. Maybe you didn't know it, but our little friend did some talking around there—or did you know it?"

"What little friend?"

"Now pictures I gotta draw! Your charity patient, Doc. Who else? Snuffy the dishwasher."

"How would you know if he did any talking? Lauziere was his only friend—at least Lauziere was the one who took care of him."

"He had a lotta friends back there. My girl's in the line at the club. Old Snuffy was loopy—and he was lonesome. The kid used to go back and talk to him. He knew *what* was wrong and he knew *who* was wrong in that bunch. He also knew how *somebody* could make a hell of a lot of moola out of his information." Dahl leaned back and took a deep sigh for himself—like he'd finished a job. "So you see, Doc, when you start prowling the little guy's room, I got more ideas than I can read in the papers. Did you get what you were looking for?"

"I was looking for Snuffy Goddard."

The man laughed. "Hell of a place to look for him!"

"In his room?"

"In a last year's *Racing Form!*" He laughed hard.

"So you were there."

"What do *you* think?" Tough this time.

"I don't think much of it, Dahl. You've got a lot of guts to admit it."

"That's for laughs, Doc, coming from you. It's all right for you to walk into a sick friend's room through an open door—but if I do it I'm a wrong guy. You couldn't prove any part of it, anyway, so what's the use of clowning around?"

"I ought to run you over to Fifty-fourth Street and have some tough cop slap it out of you."

"Ought to? Maybe you ought to, at that, pal—but you won't." He put his hat on his head and got, up. I got up with him—but quick.

"Why won't I?" I guess I barked it out. He didn't scare any. He laughed and made me sorer than ever.

"I oughtta not come up here tonight either, Doc—but I did. What we oughtta do and what we're gonna do in a spot like this don't have much to do with each other. We both got the same reason for doing like we're gonna do instead of like we oughtta do." He put up his hand in an impatient sort of way—as if to brush off any answer I might make. "Don't go into your act, fella. You may be sore as hell at me, but it ain't because you stand for law and order. If you'd've come in that room and looked for the guy and just gone out—like any doctor on the errand you say you was on—I'd've never opened my yap. But you didn't, see?" He walked past me toward the hall. I could have slugged him as he went by. "You wasn't looking for any medical information in a last year's *Racing Form* any more than I was looking for bedbugs in his mattress." Dahl might say more, so I held onto myself. He grinned as though, now that I'd been exposed, we were pals. "Look, Doc. I never been a big shot like you. I've always had to fool around with the little stuff—the soft touches. This time I got lucky. I started kickin' an idea around and found I'd run into a good one—a big one. So I find you in there. I got no right to squawk. Neither have you. It's still big."

"So you think it's big enough for both of us."

"You oughtta know, pal. I don't have to tell you." He had a quick, puzzled look for an instant.

"How do you propose to handle it? Have you got some sort of a plan worked out?" I tried to keep it solid. Maybe I didn't because the guy peered into my face again, as if he were trying to remember my name.

"You know, Doc, you ain't saying exactly the right things."

"I don't get you."

"You talk as if maybe you *didn't* know just what you're talkin' about—and there's some kind of a chance that you don't. I ain't takin' that chance. I spoke my piece." He opened the door and turned in the doorway. "But there's one thing I don't want no mistakes about. If you do know what this is all about, you know that you can't get away with it if I holler—and I can't get away with it if you do. One way or another, I cut myself in."

"Okey, Dahl. You've spoken your piece. Now how about getting out of here so I can open a window?"

He came up with a nasty leer as he turned into the hall. "Yeah. Yeah, Doc, that's a hell of an idea! It did get a little stuffy in there, didn't it!"

I stood in the doorway listening to the elevator and trying to sum up the things I knew about this strange situation in which a hoodlum like Patsy Dahl could involve himself in the lives of people like Rick Fogan, Rita Asher, and Tom Bradford.

Even Lauziere, for all his glowering, resentful feelings about the others, seemed a considerable cut above dealing with Dahl.

It was at that moment that the ghost of Snuffy Goddard began to play his part in the ill-assorted cast. Snuffy—the little man who had apparently known or possessed something of importance; the little man who had washed dishes for an occasional few dollars handed to him by Lauziere; the little man who had conveniently—for somebody, certainly—crawled back into his hole to die.

Had the others been looking for him? If they had, I hadn't heard about it. The only people who seemed to have any interest whatever in Snuffy's whereabouts were Patsy Dahl and Maggie Marra.

One thing seemed very sure. If the dishwasher had talked—said things that had given Dahl his lead—he had probably said them to others. I called Maggie at the apartment. She hadn't left for the club, yet, and said she had time to talk.

"Of course you've heard about Snuffy, Maggie."

"Yes. I read about it in the papers. I felt like the devil about getting you into that. Are you all right?"

"Perfectly, thanks. Only it wasn't prowlers as it said in the papers."

She hesitated an instant. "Wasn't prowlers, Doc?"

"Definitely not casual prowlers, anyway."

"Anybody we know?"

"Not exactly—not in our social set, that is. Listen, Maggie, what could Snuffy have known—or had in his possession—that might have been extremely important to anybody connected with the club?"

"Oh, Lord! That doesn't make sense. The poor little fellow never had anything that anybody would want. He just sat out there in back and did his work. Whenever he had time he'd talk with us—about all sorts of things."

"Never about the people in the club?"

She thought this over. "No, Doc. Maybe he'd make little cracks like the rest of us once in a while. You know, 'The boss is raising hell tonight, ain't he!' and that sort of thing." There was a moment of silence in my receiver. "Wait a minute, Doc. Would something like this mean anything? Remember the night we all had some drinks and Rick Fogan stormed out into the kitchen—I mean the night I told you about?"

"I remember what you said—Snuffy hiding the bottle under the sink . . ."

"All right. After Rick turned up in the kitchen looking for Lauziere, remember that I told you that Snuffy was a little drunk and when Eve Tillory made a crack about 'What goes on?' Snuffy told her that when she got as old as he was she'd know better than to ask questions—that it wasn't always healthy to know the answers?"

"I remember. I've thought a lot about it since."

"He said something else that night, Doc. I thought it was drunken babble—maybe it wasn't. Let's see if I can get it straight. I was a touch swacked myself. It was just before the last show—we did four that night. Everybody was pooped and the chorus dressing room was colder than your aunt Bessie's root cellar. The Tillory kid—she's a squawker by nature anyway—was blowing off in the kitchen where we were trying to get warm. She said something about she must be dumb or something—that it gave her a pain in the fanny to go out on that floor and break a leg four times a night while her guy sat out there where it was warm drinking good scotch. Well, Snuffy looked at her a little and said something like, 'Listen, Little Eva, I could be out there drinkin' good scotch, too, if I chose. They'd bring me all I wanted—on the house. You don't believe that, do you?' Eve said she didn't and called him an old rumdum. Snuffy cackled, 'Well, it's true. You girls come around askin' my advice about things, but the right people out in front, there, never done it. When they do, you won't find me washing no more dishes.' Could that mean anything, Doc?"

"In view of a lot of things that have happened since, I think it could mean a good deal. Was that all there to it?"

"That was all. We got called right after that and went on."

"Thanks, Maggie, I think maybe that's the sort of thing I've been looking for."

"Do you suppose the little feller might have had something on somebody around the place, Doc?" The big blonde gave me a telephonic grin. "Nothing short of blackmail would pry a free drink out of that layout, and when they set 'em up, it won't be for the dishwasher."

"I think you're probably right. Goddard could have had something on one of them—Lauziere, Fogan, Rita. By the way—who was Eve's scotch-drinking boy friend?"

"A very nasty guy, Doc—a heel by the name of Patsy Dahl that nobody in the place could stand."

"On thinking it over—considering the Tillory girl's hanging around Snuffy and all that—do you think the dirt might have been on Dahl?"

Maggie puzzled a moment. "You know? Maybe you've got something there. Eve was always diggin' at Snuffy for something or other. She would have been doing it for Dahl, wouldn't she!"

"That's what I had in mind." I also had in mind some very strenuous digging that Dahl had done for himself.

"I gotta go to work—but I'll tell you one thing, Doc. If they'd found a knife in Goddard's chest instead of pneumonia, I'd of known damned well it was Dahl."

10

Next day, around eleven, I got the expected call from Pop Asher. He telephoned and came up, about fifteen minutes later, wearing his Sunday suit. I was making some coffee and set out an extra cup.

"Sugar, Pop?"

"I take it just plain, thank ye kindly."

"Tom Bradford tells me you've quit him."

Thc old man studied my face until I took refuge in my coffee cup. When he'd decided where I stood in the matter, he spoke.

"Yes, I quit Tom."

Between carefully loading and lighting his pipe and drinking half a cup of coffee, Pop killed off enough time to force a question out of me. "Did you know about my interest in what happened out there, Pop? Is that why you dropped by this morning?"

"That's part of it, Doc. You're a good hand with a horse and I guess I've learned some in my fifty years with 'em. I figgered we could talk without too much backin' and fillin'."

"We can talk straight as you want to, old-timer—only I guess you know that Tom's a pretty good friend of mine . . ."

The faded blue eyes brightened up. "If he wasn't, I wouldn't be here right now. Maybe you don't know, but I about half raised the boy."

"He's told me, Pop. He and Rita more or less grew up together, didn't they?"

"That's right. Summertimes, leastways. They were great kids around the race track. Growin' up has cost both of 'em right dearly."

I didn't make any comment and the man threw me an intent, approving look before he went on. "They've both got into bad company, Doc—real bad company."

"On the track or off?"

"Off the track. That's natural. You couldn't fool either of 'em about wrong people around horses from the time they were ten." Asher's lean, leather face was eager in the defense of his memories—then stern again. "But with this sort of people they haven't got a chance."

I knew what he meant, but he told me anyway. "They were raised to know the difference between the only two kinds of people we've got in the horse business—the best in the world and the worst. . . . I can't just exactly say it . . ."

"The solid colors, Pop—not the shades."

"That's it, the solid colors—the chestnuts, the bays, and the blacks. Even the grays, Doc—the Royal Canopys—you know 'em first time you see 'em."

"But lots of every kind are common."

"Sure! Sure they're common. But they're common in a way you can understand, man! When a horse cheats, every horseman in the park knows it. When a man cheats, he fixes it up to look good."

"See here, Pop, what makes you think the people around Tom and Rita are cheating?" The disdain in his eyes was quick and sharp. "Or is that backing and filling?"

He sighed the long, unsatisfactory breath of the aged. "Doc, I've seen a lot of young horses die in their stalls and I've yet got to see one die without a struggle of some kind. I made too many beds not to know how a horse lies—or dies. They might have fooled Tom, but they didn't fool me—or you."

"They didn't fool Tom either."

The old fellow fumbled for matches in places where his Sunday suit didn't provide pockets. I tossed him a box of wooden ones. "I wouldn't have thought Tom would be taken in much—

except for his tryin' to pull the dead mare's head up with a halter. Seemed kind of dumb."

"Tom hadn't touched that halter and shank, Pop. That's the way he found it—lying right there."

Asher's pipe gurgled while he thought this over. "Yes, that's the way it would've been. I'm relieved in my mind."

"Why relieved?"

"I'll tell you why, Doc. Because I run into somebody on the place that night. I was afraid it was Tom."

I wanted to bay like a hound. "Tell me about it."

"I went to a picture show that night over on the boulevard and then set around the Trackside Bar fannin' old times with some of the boys until pretty near midnight. Bein' as it was late, I figgered to sleep in the tack room instead of goin' home." Pop occupied himself with his pipe for a moment. "Maybe I was a little drunk."

"But you came back to the barn?"

"That I did—the short way. There's a little gate between the barns and the big manure pit. It's never locked except durin' the race meeting."

"When was this, Pop?"

"As I calc'late it now, it was maybe quarter past twelve. Bert Mills, the watchman, was having his supper."

"Did he see you?"

"No. I asked him, after, if he'd noticed anybody around that night and he said he hadn't. I walked around the back side of our barn and seen a light in the mare's stall. It went out right as I come toward the shed and a fella stood up and looked in my direction."

"Could you make out who it was?"

"I guess not, Doc. I s'posed it was Tom. He's been doin' a lot of worryin', lately, and hangs around the barn all kinds of hours."

"You didn't show yourself, then?"

"Hell, no! Tom don't like for me to drink anything. He'd have fired me right then and there. I went out the back gate and on home."

"So you didn't know what had happened until next morning."

"That's right. I guess you can see how I felt about it."

"Of course, Pop. Tell me. What's Tom been worrying about?"

"Money, Doc. He hasn't been doin' too good for a while. Fogan's string was the first break he'd got in a year or so. I don't know, but I hear he owes a lot of folks a lot of money."

"That's a pretty good reason he wouldn't kill his best filly, isn't it!"

"The boy wouldn't do a thing like that for any reason I can think of. He just ain't that sort."

"Tom hasn't got much use for Fogan, has he?"

"No more have I—but Tom's got a head on his shoulders and he uses it. The way he was set up, he couldn't be very choosy whose horses he trained. It was Rita put him in with Fogan, though, and he didn't like that part of it."

I held up saying anything about Rita's regard for Fogan—or anything about her at all, for that matter. Sooner or later the whole mess would have to make some sort of sense. Time enough then. Pop lit his pipe again and added the burned match to a neat pile on the table.

"There's something else, Doc—the main thing I come to tell you. There *was* somebody I saw that night."

"In the stable area?"

"No. Outside. I stopped back in the Trackside for a nightcap and as I come out he was just gettin' into a car that was parked about twenty yards from the saloon. It's been fifteen, sixteen years since I seen him, but I recognized him right off."

"Who was it, Pop?"

"It was this feller Lozeer—I found out yesterday he's in with Fogan."

This time I did bay like a hound. "Lauziere! Are you sure it was Lauziere?"

"Dead sure. He used to be short-order cook around the track kitchens years ago. I knew him as Phil, but remembered he had some kind of funny last name. Jimmy Wallis told me yesterday he'd got to be a big shot."

I was damned and said so. Then I asked the old man if he'd ever run into a Snuffy Goddard in his travels. He watched a couple of puffs of smoke drift through the sunlight from the window.

"Not by that name, Doc—not the Snuffy part of it. There used to be a rider named Goddard a long time back. Natural light boy that could make a hundred three or four. Paddy, his name was, Paddy Goddard."

So there it was. Patrick—Paddy—Goddard. The little man, Snuffy. The little man who could have sat in the warm room and had good scotch—on the house, the little man who had said it wasn't always safe to know the answers, the little man whose wraith drove me to the telephone, after Pop had left, to call Dr. Bardon, the only witness, I supposed, to his death. Bardon said come over any time and I left at once. His office hours wouldn't start until two o'clock.

He was young, serious, and very professional. I introduced myself. "My name's Connor. I'm a physician."

"Come in, won't you, Doctor, and sit down?"

"I'd like to bother you a couple of minutes, if I may."

"No bother at all, Doctor. If there's anything I can do, I'll be happy to be of service. Glad you called when you did. I have a breathing spell just about now."

I sat in the customers' chair. "A few days ago a friend asked me to try to do something for a man who was apparently seriously ill the last time she saw him. He was broke and didn't know anybody. When I got around to his place I found that he'd died—and that you had seen him. I wonder if you'd mind telling me something about it so that I may report back. His name was Patrick Goddard."

Bardon leaned back in his chair and tapped the end of his nose with a pencil. "Yes. I remember the case very well. I'll be glad to tell you what I can—there isn't too much. I saw the man only twice . . . but here; let me get the card." He shuffled through the file and brought it out. "How much detail do you want, Doctor?"

"I don't know—exactly. Just tell me about it, if you will."

"Well, a woman named Schatz called me one morning. She runs a lodging house—a tenement, actually—down the street. She said that the man who lived in the basement room had been extremely ill and that she thought he might have pneumonia. Mrs. Schatz asked me to see him—on a charity basis, of course. When I got there Goddard was in a semi-comatose condition. He roused enough to tell me he had no money and no living relatives. When I assured him he'd be taken care of he seemed relieved. He said he'd been ill for a week or so but had blamed it on a chronic sinusitis he'd had for years."

"Could be why they called him Snuffy."

"Snuffy. Yes. Of course." He pounded his nose some more with the pencil while he justified this logic.

"What did you find?"

"On examination of the nose and throat, I found the mucosa to be violently inflamed. There were ulcerated lesions of the septum and throat. There were also indications of a severe otitis and, considering his temperature—103.4 at that hour of the morning—I naturally suspected mastoid and, possibly, lateral sinus involvement."

"Which, I'd suppose, led to your statement that a generalized septicemia was the cause of death."

"Yes, Doctor. That and a great deal more led me to the conclusion. I found distinct, characteristic moist rales in his chest. He coughed constantly and his sputum was blood-streaked. In view of the rest of the picture, wouldn't those indicia have led you to suspect a metastatic pneumonitis?"

"I—er—hope so, Doctor. I've been rather out of things for a couple of years."

The fire of the zealot burned in the boy's eyes. "Or a septopyemia?"

"Gracious!"

"What did you say, sir?"

"I said, 'Gracious!' I think. Any lymphatic enlargement?"

"Profound. Very definite."

"How about his heart?"

Bardon looked a little hurt with my interruptions. "I was coming to that, Dr. Connor. The man showed every evidence of myocardial weakness—rapid, feeble, irregular pulse—even some evidences of cyanosis."

"So what did you do then?"

"I attempted to make immediate hospital arrangements for the patient—it's very difficult, these, days, with our limited facilities for charity cases. I did find, however, that I could get him admitted the following evening, so I left instructions with Mrs. Schatz for his care in the meantime. Before I left, I administered 300,000 units of procaine penicillin, intramuscularly. I never leave the office without it."

"Admirable! You keep very well equipped, Dr. Bardon."

"I am of the opinion, Dr. Connor, that no man should enter the practice of medicine without the finest of equipment—material and mental."

I was a little floored by it all. "Come to think of it, that seems very practical." I tried to remember if I'd ever been that way. Probably not. The Old Doc would have ridden me out of town on a rail. But then the Old Doc was something else again. I had a warm feeling for this youngster with all his bright, new weapons and his gallant faith in them. I wondered how many of the cards in his well-filled case file were blank. Maybe I felt a little old. Older than my pretty well preserved thirty-five, anyway.

"The next afternoon, some time before I had arranged for the ambulance to arrive, Mrs. Schatz called me and said that the man seemed to be dying. I hurried over and, although I have seldom found a layman to be correct in such a case, Mrs. Schatz was not in error."

"Goddard was dying?"

"The patient was exhibiting terminal symptoms when I arrived. On noting his cyanotic appearance, I immediately suspected—and found—a condition of advanced pulmonary edema accompanied by substantial evidence of cardiac collapse. Naturally I hurriedly instituted such therapeutic measures as I could."

"Gracious!"

"What did you say, sir?"

"I'm afraid I said, 'Gracious!' again. I hope you'll forgive me." Bardon looked at me intently. I'm certain he was reviewing his Psych. 10, Abnormal, North Hall, Mon-Wed-Fri., Dr. Glisch.

"Of course."

"Then what therapeutic measures did you institute?"

"Strophanthin and atropine, of course. The patient did not rally sufficiently to justify my leaving his side. A few minutes later he was *in extremis* and I made the routine attempts to stimulate some further cardiac response with coramine—but it was impossible. I called the authorities."

"I don't see how anyone could have done more, Dr. Bardon. I'm certain my friend will be happy that Goddard had every attention." I got up and found my hat. Somewhere in the back of my professional department a small bell tinkled. A lecture came back to me. An exposition on a subject which was to be of almost no concern to the physician of the future. A lecture in May—with the windows open and the sounds of early summer outside. "Before I go, there are a couple of things I'm rather curious about. The first is a professional question. Did you find any external lesions on the body?"

"None that I could readily relate to the patient's condition, Dr. Connor. As I remember, however, there were a few acne-like pustular lesions around the bridge of his nose. On second thought, they might occur, of course, in such a septicemia, mightn't they!"

The little bell rewarded me with quite a healthy jangle. "They might, indeed, Doctor. Now, if you will, did the patient, at any time, say anything more about himself? I have reason to believe that Goddard could have been in some trouble—wondered if he might have said something to suggest what it was."

"Let me think." Bardon wandered around the office and wound up at the desk. He reclaimed his pencil and beat himself on the nose with it again. "I can't recall anything he said that would be significant. There was once when he rallied a little from the strophanthin he muttered something. It didn't make any sense."

"It might make sense to me. What was it?"

"Well, as nearly as I can make out he was trying to blame some woman for his troubles."

"Is that irrational?"

"I don't know to what degree it was or wasn't rational, Doctor, but the man said something like 'It's on her account, it's on her account.' He didn't speak again. Does that make sense to you?"

"Frankly, it doesn't—at the moment. It will before I'm done digging around."

"Digging around? I trust you don't mean that literally, Doctor."

"I don't, actually—but it's a hell of an idea, come to think of it. Listen, Bardon. What would you say if I told you that Goddard had spent his life with horses?"

"Horses?" The youngster came up with an extraordinarily convincing slow take. "Horses!" He gave his nose three stern slugs with the pencil. "Why—I'd—I'd—*gracious!*"

"What did you say?"

His eyebrows went up to their extreme capacity. "I'm afraid I said, 'Gracious,' Doctor. I must read up again on this! I was assured I'd never have occasion—*gracious!* . . ."

He must have looked funny to his afternoon patients with his eyebrows up like that. Certainly I did nothing to take them down.

11

I don't know how much reading up young Dr. Bardon did, that afternoon, but I did a lot of it. I even hustled over to the library to supplement my lagging loose-leaf encyclopedia of medicine. An odd, bad pun hit me as I climbed the broad steps from Fifth Avenue—something about reading between the lions. There was plenty of that to be done too.

I plowed through files and records with a fervor I hadn't known for years, strengthening my hunch, as the afternoon wore on, that an ancient enemy of man had come back, practically from its grave, to scratch Snuffy Goddard from the rolls. Throughout the recorded history of medicine, *Bacilli mallei* have emerged from their dark breeding places to destroy horses —and people. Once established in the blood stream of either, they march, unchecked, through their almost inevitable cycle of delirium, convulsions, coma, and death. In their fight against extinction *Bacilli mallei* are said, on top authority, to have killed more laboratory workers than any other organism.

I got one of the veterinary staff of the Department of Agriculture on the phone before he left his office. Yes, the incidence of the disease, glanders, was extremely low among the horse population of this country; elsewhere too. The Department no longer sees the need for the mallein test on imported stock. In humans? Did you ever see a case, Doctor? When I told him I hadn't—but thought I knew a physician who had, he said the Department would be very much interested. Would I be able to locate a case of animal glanders which might have been discovered within the last six weeks? Undoubtedly. They are brought immediately to the attention of state and federal authorities. I thanked him with a lot on my mind.

If Snuffy Goddard had died, as I believed, from glanders, he had hit the longest price of the century in the daily double of death. Somewhere, not too far away, there had been a glanderous animal—reported or unreported—within the last month or so. The animal would be dead as Snuffy was dead, but at some time during that period they would have been together. Or would they?

The fact that the little man died so conveniently for at least one of a group of people who knew so much about horses kept fouling up my thinking. He'd possessed something—or known something—that several of those people apparently wanted for themselves. Once shucked of his secret, Goddard would be tossed aside like the husk from an ear of field corn.

After a lot of dabbling around with the limitations of culture media, temperature tolerances, and what not, I set out for dinner with a fixed conclusion in my mind. Either Goddard had been handling a glanderous animal ten days or so before his death or he had been within easy reach of someone who had. To someone who was troubled by Snuffy's presence in the world, the discovery of the diseased horse—plus fifteen minutes with an old horseman's manual—would have seemed a providential solution to his problem.

Perhaps of secondary interest to the killer would be the fact that, while he might not be committing the first murder of its kind in history, it was a million to one that he was committing the last.

I decided to eat at the Ricky Club.

It was a little early and I sat up at the bar for a drink. The bartender set out the Old Forester and minded his own business. I was heavily engaged in minding mine when Lauziere came up—scrubbed and inscrutable.

"Good evening, Doctor. Are you in search of Olympia oysters tonight? Or possibly something more—substantial?"

I suppose it was I knew too much about the guy, but I couldn't get over the impression he wanted to play games. I dealt myself in.

"I don't know what I'm in search of, Philippe. Maybe you can suggest something."

"Very well—you shall have a suggestion at once." His smile could have gone with a birthday present. "Since I find myself more alert during the evening if I do not eat dinner, I reserve the next half hour for a drink and a canapé Russe in my office. Will you join me, Doctor?"

I allowed as how with such finesse as came to hand and trailed him through the long hall to a pleasant enough room furnished with a plain desk, three or four comfortable chairs, and about a hundred horse pictures—photographs of finishes, mostly, with dates like 1934. I didn't stare, but Lauziere said:

"You see, we have a common interest, Doctor. Won't you sit down?"

I muttered something about horses and found a chair. A waiter came in with a tray of stuff including my Forester bottle. The canapé was peerless—and Russe to the extent of providing caviar that stayed black. I was just about to forget, for the moment, that my host was probably a horse killer when he opened the meeting. He might as well have rapped for order—it was that fast.

"I was sorry to hear of your misfortune the other night. It was, I understand, in connection with a man who had been working in the kitchen here."

"It was. I'd heard he was ill—some of the girls in the show were concerned—so I went out to see if I could do anything for him."

Lauziere clucked with sympathy and understanding—with a small, mocking smile thrown in to keep me amused. ". . . and you were attacked!"

"You can call it that." The guy was about as expert in handing out a slow burn as he'd proved dishing out food. "There were a couple of guys there ahead of me."

"From the appearance of your head, Dr. Connor, I feel certain that at least one of them was—er—behind you, also." We laughed merrily at this and I felt a sudden wave of pity for the girls in the line. Their Let's-Louse-Up-Lauziere Club had a new member. The guy tossed down a brace of caviars, poured himself a fresh cocktail, and waved at my whisky bottle. "Come, come! Help yourself, sir."

I did. "Thanks."

"I had been wondering if you have felt any concern for our ex-dishwasher—beyond that for his physical welfare."

Now he was really getting on with his agenda. "Concern, Lauziere? Why should I have had any concern for the man?"

"I haven't the slightest idea—not the slightest." He spread his hands. The gesture could have been Gallic. On the other hand, it could have been for the funny papers. "There have been a number of things happening to us here that I can't explain. I thought, perhaps wrongly, that you might have interested yourself in them."

I felt sure that, considering the relationship between Fogan and Lauziere, any knowledge this, fellow had of Rick's problems had not come from headquarters. I also felt sure that in any sort of a friendly conspiracy I'd come off second best. I played it dumb. "I was a little puzzled by the fact that even the lowest-class prowler would have been interested in the man's pitiful quarters. Did you know Goddard, by the way?"

The man beamed égalité, fraternité and what I took to be plain, personal malignance. "I knew him by sight many years, ago when he was exercise boy and part-time jockey. I was, at the time, a grease jockey in the track kitchens. We have come and gone far, have we not, he and I?"

"There's no doubt about the fact that he's gone far, anyway. How come he turned up here?"

"There I am mystified. Will you have a cigar?"

"Not now, thanks."

"I have not seen this fellow for many years. Not since the days when I spent a great deal of time at the race track. Now, of a sudden, he turns up asking for work. He has no money, he has no proper clothing—he has nothing. Yet tough people try to rob his room. I am most definitely curious—I could not blame you for being the same."

"You wouldn't have any idea, would you, Lauziere, who tried to rob his room?"

"But no, of course!" He didn't seem disturbed, at that.

"Nor why?"

"Naturally not!" He folded his hands carefully across his small, hard belly and added, "Have you?"

"No idea whatever." I decided to venture further and see what happened. "Tell me, Philippe, have these—shall we say—small incidents—led you to the conclusion that anything is seriously wrong?"

For the first time Lauziere seemed to pull his attention away from the refreshments and gave it entirely to me. "The incidents, as you describe them, include some of which you know and some of which you don't. By themselves they could be unimportant. On the other hand, Doctor, if they are related, they could suggest a . . . most unpleasant situation."

". . . and you think they are related?" I wanted to add "or do you simply want to know if I think so"—which seemed much more to the point. Lauziere went back to the canapé.

"Personally, I do not know anything about it. I am convinced that my partner does, however—and is very much disturbed."

"Your partner?"

"Fogan."

"I'm sorry—I didn't . . ."

"A natural mistake, Doctor. It is better for the patrons that the maître is not known as one of the owners." He pushed his plate away with a small sigh. "You are forgiven. Take absolution from your bottle."

"Thanks, Philippe. I think I shall punish myself by refusing this time." A handful of quick ideas sorted themselves out in my mind. The partners' mutual distrust would bar confidential exchanges completely. To Lauziere, I seemed to be in the confidence of Fogan. Now I was being invited to swap ideas with Lauziere. All I need now, I thought, is to have Rick Fogan suspect me of playing little games with his partner! I decided to wrap up the interview and get the hell out of there.

"I'm afraid I'm a little out of my depth in all this, Philippe. I've known Tom Bradford for some time and was glad to do what I could about the mare—which was nothing at all. My call at Goddard's place was simply the outgrowth of that. I hadn't even met Maggie Marra before. I know nothing which would tend to connect the incidents in my mind." My reference to the mare didn't pay off.

"You are not even curious to know who banged you over the head?" Lauziere's tone implied that he was somewhat concerned for my sanity.

"No. I'm no longer curious. You see, I . . ." I heard the door open behind me, but couldn't stop what I was saying. I'd wanted to say it ever since I'd come into the office. ". . . you see, I know who banged me over the head."

The face of the man across the desk went sick-yellow. I couldn't tell whether it was from my statement or from what he saw back of me. I turned around. Rick Fogan was standing with his hand on the doorknob. His face was set and angry. He stared at Lauziere steadily for a moment before he spoke—hard, quiet, stiff-jawed.

"You're needed out on the floor, Phil. At once."

"Yes." He rose slowly with all his hatred in his eyes. "Yes, of course, Rick. I'd been chatting with the doctor and hadn't noticed the time. You'll excuse me, Dr. Connor?"

I told him of course or something and watched him leave. Fogan stood aside as Lauziere approached the door. Their eyes met again, for an instant, as Philippe passed through. You could hear it. Fogan closed the door and stood with his back to it. I swung around in my chair. "Well, Doc?"

"Would that mean that explanations are in order?"

Fogan walked slowly around the desk and sat down. "Tom Bradford told me you'd agreed to forget the trouble at the barn."

"That's right."

"Then why investigate Phil Lauziere?"

"I wasn't investigating Lauziere. He was investigating me."

The man's face was tense. Angry. "Perhaps you'll tell me why?"

"That doesn't make sense. How the hell would I know why Lauziere wants to pump me?" I felt I was being pushed around and didn't like it.

"Did he ask you to come here?"

"No. You ask people to come here in the newspapers. I didn't have any particular reason to come. I just came." I guess I hollered.

"All right, Doc—don't get sore. Lauziere's trying to make trouble. He never misses a chance to embarrass me."

"Do you feel like telling me why, Rick?"

"It's simple enough. He wants the business."

"You once told me he didn't have much left in it."

"He hasn't—at the moment—but the club has some obligations to meet and Lauziere will have to dig up some cash. We both will."

I wondered about Lauziere digging up cash. "Has he got it, Rick?"

Fogan laughed without smiling. "Unfortunately, he's got a lot of it. I put up the major part of the stake when we opened here. He took a smaller piece of the business and held onto his money."

"Why unfortunately?"

"Because, unless I can raise the cash elsewhere, Lauziere's got me over a barrel. We're just beginning to operate on a paying basis—much slower than I expected. When we were doing extremely well, right at first, I committed myself for the horses and some other investments. Then we hit the doldrums and I had to extend myself pretty far."

"So, now that the business is secure and profitable, your partner is quite willing to buy you out!" The smooth Philippe's gestures may not have been truly Gallic, but his business acumen was.

"That's it, Doc. At least that's the way Lauziere *thinks* it is." Fogan gave me a hard smile. "But he's a long way from being top man around here yet! I'm not an easy person to take things away from."

"But, in the meantime, he's being unpleasant as hell."

"Exactly." Fogan looked at the remains of the canapé and shoved the tray away from him. "I heard you telling Lauziere you knew who hit you over the head."

"I do."

"Who was it?"

"Want to make a deal, Rick?"

"What sort of a deal?" He lit a cigarette and grinned through the smoke at me. "I'm always open for a deal that'll do me some good."

"This deal might do you a lot of good. Suppose you convince Bradford that no right people are going to get hurt if I nose around a little more in the matter of the trouble at the barn."

"Oh?" He had to think about that a moment. "Suppose I do—then?"

"Then I tell you quite a lot of things you don't know yet."

"Such as?"

"Such as who the guy was that conked me."

The tall man leaned over the desk toward me. "What'll that get me?"

"It'll get you the privilege of making a more intelligent guess as to why somebody killed your filly."

"That doesn't tie up."

"I think it does—but you'll at least be in a position to tell whether it does or not when you know who's dealt himself in."

Fogan's voice was sharp. "Into what?"

"I have no idea." I thought of Dahl's trip to Rick's empty office. "Certainly something that concerns you."

"Look, Doc, I don't think I'm interested. The filly's dead and whoever destroyed her has the satisfaction of knowing it hurt me. I'm damned if I give him the satisfaction of seeing me involved in a scandal. Let it drop."

"You haven't heard the whole deal yet. I told you I thought it would do you some good."

"So what's the rest?"

"The rest is that I can come pretty close to telling you who killed the mare."

"The hell you can!"

"I think so, Rick. He was at the track shortly after twelve that night."

"Who, Doc? For the love of God—who?"

"Lauziere."

Fogan stood up and stared over my head at the closed door. His knuckles were white-pressed on the desk top, his face rigid as his body.

"Lauziere!"

12

After a bad few minutes with Fogan while he backed me to the door, saying incomprehensible things and staring over my shoulder, I went home and opened a friendly can of chile.

All in all, I was pretty well pleased with my four days of nosing around café society. I had everybody going through everybody else's pockets, at least, which would hold them a day or so while I looked up a case of glanders. I felt morally certain there had been one.

If Snuffy Goddard had died from the disease, he had been infected not more than ten days or two weeks before his death. He died on March ninth. Two weeks back of that was February twenty-third.

I looked up Mrs. Schatz in the phone book without much hope of finding a number. It was there—Schatz, Josie, Apts. 1410 Harker. After some fumbling around, Mrs. Schatz said that Goddard had rented the room on February twenty-seventh in the afternoon. He had paid two weeks rent in advance and had apparently brought no belongings with him. I thanked her and got my desk calendar from the office. Snuffy had moved in on the twenty-seventh and he had died ten days later.

Giving him the benefit of a fairly slow incubation period—which can be very fast, sometimes—Goddard must have been infected very close to the day he checked into Mrs. Schatz's place. Within a day, say.

How long had he worked at the club? It took a lot of fooling around, but I finally got Maggie Marra on the phone.

"Snuffy? Oh, Doc, I couldn't say. He wasn't there long, actually, but you spend a lot of hours together in this business and we had a good many laughs with the old fella."

"How long would you guess he'd worked there?"

"Lemme see! Two weeks? Maybe less than that. I remember one thing, though. He turned up with an old paper suitcase and a couple of packages and left them in one of the dressing rooms. He asked me about that. It was the first time I talked to him—said he was going to look around for a room the next day. I think he slept in the back of the club that night."

"That does it, Maggie, thanks! Do you remember if he might have slept in the club the next night?"

"No. Come to think of it, Doc, I believe he said he had found a room that night when he came to work."

"But he didn't take his stuff away."

"He took it out of the dressing room, but I believe he kept it at the club. He changed his clothes out back someplace."

"Maggie, listen! Would you like to do something for the little guy that gave you the laughs? Sort of a last service to his memory?"

"Are you kidding?"

"I'm very much in earnest. Find that stuff of Goddard's—Snuffy's—I'm sure it'll be around there someplace. Just locate it. Don't touch it. Don't examine it. Above all, kid, don't get caught looking for it."

"You do sound serious. Is there something unpleasant going on?"

"There's something *very* unpleasant going on, Maggie. Take my word for it. Don't take any chances like asking where the stuff is. Just snoop around when you can and don't let anybody catch you doing it."

"I'll call you if I locate it, Doc."

I hung up and got back to my calendar. Snuffy must have arrived from someplace on the twenty-sixth of February. It could have been from Hackensack or it could have been from Montreal.

But wherever he'd arrived from, there'd been a glanderous horse if my guess was any good. I went to sleep, that night, as pleased as a pup with an old shoe.

It was a funny thing. Very unusual. The horses wouldn't break out of the gate. They were lined up and the man said, "Come on!" and the bell rang. But they didn't break. Mr. Fitz walked over and said he saw that happen once in Baltimore and maybe he'd better start them. So he rang the bell and hollered, "Come on!" and they still wouldn't start. Well, I never saw Mr. Fitz so mad. He rang . . . and rang . . . and rang . . .

"Doc! This is Maggie."

I found the phone in my hand. "Yes? Maggie? Oh. What about it?"

"I've located the stuff. Snuffy's suitcase and things."

"Swell. Wait a minute. What time is it?"

"It's something after four-thirty. I stayed until we'd closed. Fooled around mending costumes. There's nobody here."

"Why can't I look them over right now? Are you too tired to stay there a few minutes?"

"Hell, no, Doc. This is exciting. I'll wait for you just inside the stage door—come in through the alley. There's a light."

"Okey, Maggie. Good girl! I'll be there in twelve minutes. By the way. Where'd you find the stuff?"

"Lemme do my own routine, buster! I've got a surprise for you that'll knock your ears down. I don't want to tell it to you, I want to show it to you. You said something nasty is going on around here? Well, I looked in the nastiest place I could think of, and there it was! Come on! Get on your horse!"

I was in a cab in five minutes and, in another three or four, was paying off at the mouth of the alley back of the club. I couldn't see the light Maggie had said would be over the door, so I groped around until I located kitchen smells. I followed the wall along and came to a doorway. My pencil flash showed me: "Ricky—Stage & Deliveries."

I pushed the door open and went in. The joint was completely dark. The flash pointed out a second door beyond. I went through. Still dark.

"Maggie!" Not a sound. I suddenly was overwhelmed with the fear that something had happened to her. My fault. My fault. Why the hell did I always have to get other people into my troubles?

"Maggie!" My shouting rolled around into the big dining room and came back to me—without locating the woman. I listened, holding my breath—then heard a step far ahead of me. Boards creaked and the steps hurried, careless of their sound. Somebody was running. It wouldn't be Maggie. I hollered:

"Hey! You! Hold it or I'll shoot!"

Shoot! Silly gesture! A window slid up. I ran forward with the small beam ahead of me—fell over a chair.

Everything was quiet again. Then a motor started up somewhere in front of the club. The car roared away in second with the accelerator on the floor boards.

"Maggie! It's Doc. Where are you?"

"Doc! Here! Dressing rooms!" It was faint. I put my light toward the voice and located a hall—followed it down. "Speak again, Maggie, where are you?"

"In here!" Closer. "In here, Doc. I'm hurt!"

I found a light switch finally and got a feeble row of bulbs down the hall.

Maggie was on the floor of one of the dressing rooms. She was bleeding from the mouth and nose and had a badly swollen cheek.

"My God, Maggie, I'm sorry. What happened? Somebody just went out ahead of me." I got her into a chair.

"I don't know what happened. Whoever you heard slugged me. Some guy!" There was a washbasin and I wet a handkerchief and daubed at her face. "I was . . . Doc! The stuff! Look under the dressing table. Back under the chintz cover. Look quick, Doc!"

I looked. There were a couple of silly-looking odds and ends under there, but nothing else. "Was the suitcase there?"

"Yes. The suitcase and some other stuff."

"It's gone, Maggie." She began to cry. "To hell with it. Let's get you straightened out first and then talk."

"I'm all right. I want to go home." She tried to get up and sat down suddenly again. I brought her a glass of water. In return, I got a one-sided grin. "Look, Sherlock, go into my dressing room next door and get Doc Watson a spot of something that'll really do some good. It's on the shelf back of the hatbox."

It was good brandy and we each had a large palliative drink. It helped me, at least. I heard trash cans booming in the alley and realized I'd better get Maggie home. "Any idea who hit you?"

"No. I didn't hear anything. The lights were out all over the place except here in the hall and at the back. That's where I phoned you."

"In back?"

"Yes. The service phone. It's just inside the outer door."

"Then you returned to this room?"

She reclaimed her bag from the floor and stuffed my sopped handkerchief someplace in it. "I'll wash it and send it back. Thanks."

"Did you come back here after you'd phoned?"

"Yes. He must have been behind the door or something." Maggie got up—and stayed up, this time. "Let's go home, shall we, Doc?"

"Sure." I got her together and left her by the alley door while I went back and turned out the lights. On the street I stopped a cab and we headed for the Marra apartment.

"I'm terribly sorry I got you into this, Maggie. I should have known better than to suggest it." Then I thought of Danny for the first time. "Your husband will kill me!"

"Danny'll be all right. He knew we were playing cops-'n-robbers."

"He did? How?"

"We'd talked about it some after you got knocked out in Snuffy's place. I called him tonight and told him I'd be late—and why." She laughed glumly. "I told him you warned me not to get caught prowling and he tried his damnedest to get me to come home right after my last show. I told him off. Is my face terrible?"

"Not too bad. You'll need some Covermark for a day or two, though. Get some cold packs on it."

"I will." Maggie leaned back in the cab. "You know whose dressing room we were in, Doc?"

"I'd forgotten to ask. Whose was it?"

"Rita's."

"Rita Ross! The hell it was! That what you meant when you said you'd looked in the nastiest place you could think of?"

"That's right. All the trouble I've seen around the club has had something to do with her."

"How come?"

"Oh, I don't know, exactly. It isn't what's said. It's the things you feel. I'm sure that Rita's been the cause of a lot of bad feeling around the place."

"Like with Fogan and Lauziere?"

"Exactly—and with all of us. She's been sticking her nose into everybody's affairs lately and nobody likes it."

"Maybe looking for Snuffy's possessions?"

"She's been looking for something besides trouble. When you told me to try and find the suitcase, I figured she might have been after it herself."

"Apparently she was."

"Why would she be hunting for a pitiful mess of trash like that?"

"If you knew that, I think you could answer a lot of questions, Maggie. Just forget the whole thing. I suspect the gent who hit you tonight will pay off with something beside an apology."

"Such as with what, Doc?"

"Such as with his life." The cab rolled up to the apartment building. "Now don't ask me any more about it. I'll tell you what goes on. I promise."

"Okey." She felt her face tenderly and looked at her hand for blood. "Okey, Doc, but I've got a stake in this thing, now."

"Definitely you've got a stake in it. There may be some ways in which you can help me get a very handsome revenge on the guy that hit you—without taking any further chances." I told the driver to wait and saw Maggie to her door. "Better get some cold compresses on that face." She smiled with stiff muscles. "And thanks. I'm awfully sorry!" '

"It's all right, Sherlock. I'm afraid Danny will gloat. He loves to be right."

But that Saturday morning Danny wasn't doing any gloating. Maggie beckoned me inside and pointed to the open bedroom door. There on the bed with all his clothes on lay The Marra surrounded by the creolinic vapors of a Glasgow pub—out. I could have snitched his appendix without further anesthesia.

At least that's the way he looked.

13

I got a note from the government veterinarian in the morning mail. Would I call him, it had said. Brother! Would I call him! I got him at home.

"I was interested in your inquiry of yesterday, Dr. Connor, and did some asking around. You stated, rather pointedly, I thought, that you believe you know a physician who had seen a case of glanders. I took that to mean the infection of the human—and perhaps recently."

"I could be wrong, of course—but—" I didn't see any percentage in stalling around. "Well, if I'm right, you're right. The man is dead and buried."

He chuckled. "So's the horse."

"Good Lord! *What* horse? Have you located a glanderous carcass or something?"

"Actually, no. What I have located, though, is a complaint to the Department which might mean that somebody has *disposed* of a glanderous carcass. It could be a piece of malicious neighborhood squabbling, of course. We occasionally get those—dairymen accusing each other of allowing their Bang's herds to roam and that sort of thing."

"Tell me about it, Doctor." I wanted to yell. No case of glanders had been reported in two years.

"You know where Fuldenville is?"

I said I did. Fuldenville is about eighty miles south of New York in a rural area where there is some little horse breeding. It's not far from the old Bannerton race track.

"Well, they got a letter back on March first at the local Department office—they don't clear through us—to the effect that one Martin Zertic, a dealer in work horses, had concealed the fact that he'd had a case of glanders in his barn."

"Why would he have concealed it?"

"For any number of reasons. We take pretty drastic action in cases like that and make a hell of a lot of trouble for everybody concerned. We'd have quarantined all of his stock—any of it that could have been exposed—for one thing. Then we'd have run mallein tests on every horse in sight, for another. That's not too good for a dealer."

"I see. What has the Department done?"

"I'm not sure. It doesn't fall under my jurisdiction. I'm certain they've done something—at least enough to prove there's no further danger. The chances are that the period of incubation was well over before we got there."

"Why did the letter writer complain?"

"I wasn't told. Probably some guff about civic duty. It usually is. I could get you a copy of the thing in time."

"Never mind the letter. Tell me who to call and where. I think I'll run down there and have a look around."

"You can call Dr. Parkie at Bannerton 36, ring 2. Got that?"

"Right."

"Tell him I suggested you call and I think he'll give you all the co-operation you want."

"Thanks, Doctor, I'll let you know what happens."

"How about loosening up a little and letting me know what it's all about?"

"I'm trying to find out where a little guy named Goddard got a skinful of *Bacilli mallei*—and, more particularly, why."

"Well, I'll tell you one thing that's damned near sure. If your man had glanders . . ."

"He wasn't my man. He was treated by another doctor. I didn't see him at all."

The guy chuckled again ". . . if the other man's man had glanders then, he'd been in Fuldenville within a couple of weeks of his death. There hasn't been even the suspicion of it anywhere else."

I thanked him and called passenger information at the station. By three o'clock I was in Bannerton looking for a public phone. I learned from one of the lesser Parkies that the doctor was out on a call and wouldn't be back until suppertime. I found the local cab and headed for Fuldenville.

"Anyplace particular in Fulden?"

"Know a horse dealer named Zertic?"

"Old Marty? Sure." The driver took a quick left turn. "He's on the back road. Buyin'?"

"Sellin'."

The man regarded me carefully in the mirror. I was dressed in a neat, brown suit befitting of my station. Finally he said, "Oh." He drove about a mile and turned right. "Marty's got no electric."

"Is that right! Must be a backward sort of a cuss."

"I wouldn't count on that too much if it's hosses you're sellin', mister. I thought you might be peddlin' somethin' that had to have electric."

"Horses. A carload from Kansas City."

"That's a lot of hosses, a carload." He pulled into a side road and up a lane. The place was pretty broken down, but there were half a dozen head of nice work stock in the pasture. "Here y'are, mister, that'll be a dollar. Want me to come back?"

"I think you'd better wait. I'll make it right with you. I won't be long."

"I figgered I'd wait if you wanted. When you tell Marty you got a carload of hosses to sell him, you'll be all through doin' business."

As I walked up the path, a big man in overalls came out of the house and watched me without curiosity.

"Mr. Zertic?"

"One of 'em. I'm Martin. My brother's in town."

"My name is Connor and I've got some horses to sell."

"Sell, eh?" He leaned on the fence and sized me up. "Don't see many city men hoss tradin' these days." He grinned.

"Well, look me over. I'm a city man and I'm hoss tradin'. Bought a carload of work stock out of a bankruptcy sale in Kansas City. They're ready to ship and I want to move 'em."

"I can't handle no carload of horses. Whoever told you I could?"

"Man named Dahl." Zertic showed no sign of recognition. "You mean you couldn't board a carload? Maybe help me sell them?"

"Hell, yes. I kin board sixty, seventy until winter. When you figger they'll be in?"

"They'll load the horses whenever I wire. Can I look the place over?"

Zertic growled a little at that. "It's just like any other place in the farmin' country. Nothin' fancy. I feed good and I and my brother take the best care of our horses that anybody does around here."

"I was just wondering if you had a place they could be quarantined . . ."

Zertic stiffened up. Alert and angry. "Quarantined? What's wrong with 'em?"

An old Ford came down the lane. The driver pulled alongside the cab to exchange rural colloquy. "I don't know that anything's wrong with them. Don't you quarantine new stock?"

"No, I don't quarantine new stock." He said it nice and nasty. "What's more, Connor, I don't think you got any hosses." He turned and walked a few steps toward the Ford. "Jake! Come 'ere, will ye?" The car pulled up and another big man got out.

"What's the trouble?"

I said, "There's no trouble at all. I simply asked your—"

Marty hollered me down. "The hell there ain't trouble. Listen, Jake, this fella come around here talkin' about boardin' a carload of work stock. That sounded fishy enough fer a start—then he asks me about quarantines."

Jake looked at me for a moment. "He's another God damned gover'ment inspector. Look here, mister, I don't know what you want, but I kin tell you one thing—you kin go back where you come from. We got a clean bill o' health from the gover'ment. Doc Parkie was on the place two, three days."

"Why?" I decided I might as well play my hand out, anyway.

The men looked at each other in silence. Then Marty spoke up. "We know our rights, Connor. You kin either show your gover'ment papers or you kin get out. If you haven't got no gov-er'ment papers I'll damned well throw you off the place myself."

"I told you what I was here for." Jake moved toward me with a threat in every step. The guys totaled close to five hundred pounds and I wasn't giving away that kind of weight. Marty closed in until I thought I'd have to take a poke at him. He didn't talk loud then.

"Okey, Connor." He reached out a paw.

Jake said: "Wait a minute, Mart." He moved up some more. "Get goin'!"

I left. The only bit of dignity I added to my retreat was that I didn't run. I wanted to, at that. As I passed the Ford, I saw two five-gallon oilcans in the back. I remembered the Zertics had no electric.

The cab driver said nothing while I got in. As we went through the entrance I told him to turn right—circle the farm.

"You can do that. They's another lane cuts through between Zertic's place and Packer's." As we ran along the fence row I noticed a lazy cloud of blackish smoke hanging over the end of the field. When we pulled closer I could see a few wisps apparently coming from the ground. The Zertic house was disappearing behind a rise in the field. When we reached the corner I told the driver to stop, got out, and climbed through the fence. Then I knew that Jake's oilcans weren't for lighting purposes. In a gruesome barbecue pit dug deep in the ground were the remains of a tremendous fire of fence posts. It had practically burned out, but under the charred ends of the wood was a partially consumed carcass of a horse. *Bacilli mallei* are hard enough to secure from suspected material under the best conditions—certainly not from that sterilized mess. I went back to the car.

"I guess we can go now."

The driver looked over my shoulder, up the knoll. "I was figgerin' it was about time." He nodded his head in the direction of the top. Marty Zertic was walking hurriedly down the slope with a shotgun in his hand. We got out of there.

"Back to Bannerton now, mister?"

"That's right. When's the next train to New York?"

"Only one more until late tonight—four-eighteen. I meet that one ever' day. We just got time."

I made the four-eighteen and rode back to town. If I could place Goddard in Fuldenville a day or so before he turned up in New York, I'd have the source of his disease. If I could place anybody else connected with the case in Fuldenville, I'd have the killer. It's true enough that not too many horsemen have actually seen a case of glanders, but they all know about it—and it would be almost impossible not to recognize it in a horse. The symptoms are unpleasantly positive. I doubted that either the Zertics or Snuffy Goddard would have been mistaken. It was a million to one that the horse in the pit had been the only case in the United States at the time. If an old-timer like Goddard had ever seen the animal, he'd not have gone near it.

At home, I checked on Maggie, who reported that, aside from her face being a sight, she was no worse off for her adventure. Danny had boasted such a hangover that he'd done no gloating in the morning. Katie had gone to Philadelphia for the week end to play croquet or something she does several times a year with people named Lansing. I kept a call in for the Bannerton vet.

About eight-thirty Eddie Marsh banged on the door. He won't learn to use the buzzer. I got him safely into my big chair without breaking any furniture and made him a drink.

"How's your equicide?" This after he'd contemplated his feet for some three or four minutes.

"No results so far—nothing conclusive, at least. I think I know who killed the filly, but I'm damned if I can figure out why."

"That's important." He slung his head back and laughed. "That is, it would be if anybody beside a horse had been killed."

"There was."

Marsh threw one of his sudden, inquiring looks at me. "There was what?"

"There was somebody beside a horse killed." I had fun watching his big mug while he tried to figure out who was doing the kidding.

"Who got killed?"

"An ex-jockey by the name of Goddard."

"Rats!"

"Not rats, chum—even more unusual than rats."

"Rot, then!" Eddie was in it up to his neck already. "There was a perfectly sound certificate on Goddard. I checked it when I looked him up for you. Septicemia."

"Dull reading it was, too, wasn't it! Generalized septicemia, probable origin in metastic pneumonitis, et cetera, et cetera, et cetera. All very clear and all very wrong."

"What the hell do you mean? What did the guy die of, then?"

"You diagnosed it better than the doctor."

"I? Go ahead. Make me smart."

"You said, 'Rot!' just now. That's pretty close to the cause of his death. He died from a horseman's disease called glanders if my guess is any good."

". . . and our people downtown didn't know it? That's stupid!"

"Don't be too hard on your people downtown; it isn't as stupid as—"

Eddie stuck out his jaw. "I mean you're being stupid! Just because a doctor's working for the Police Department, you think—"

"I don't think anything of the kind. I'm trying to get it through your thick head that, unless the man is known to be working with horses, not one physician out of a thousand would even think of glanders. There has been exactly one case in the United States in the last two years. Goddard got tangled up with it—with the assistance of somebody I hope to turn over to you one of these days."

"Listen, Doc, are you serious? Are you trying to cook up another murder?"

"I'm strictly serious—and the murder's already been cooked up." I'd been just kidding around with the big cop up to that, but it seemed as good a time as any to get him interested—unofficially. "Naturally, Eddie, I could be wrong . . ."

"You aren't just speculating, Doc! You could be awfully wrong. You'll have to dig up a pretty clean story to get me interested. It sounds fictional."

"I'm afraid you'll have to do the digging up—sooner or later. Sooner, probably. *Bacilli mallei* resist putrefactive changes for only about thirty days. The man's been buried two weeks already."

Eddie sighed and blew out his breath. "You have just fixed me up to make a complete ass out of myself in the Department. A few of our lads have demanded exhumation orders and been very sorry they did. That's one move you've got to be right about."

"I'll be right about it, Eddie. I think things are about ready to boil over. My murderer socked a very nice lady last night for getting her nose into his business."

As Marsh was asking why it hadn't been reported, the phone rang. It was Parkie calling from Bannerton. I told him of my experience with the brothers Zertic and asked him about the letter.

"I haven't seen the letter, itself. The original was directed to Washington and a copy forwarded to me. I do all the Department work in this section—mostly cattle, of course. Hold on a minute and I'll get the copy."

The noises of the Parkie household took over the line until the vet came back to the phone . . .

"Here it is. Now what can I tell you about it?"

"Everything, if you will, Doctor. Start with the date, say."

"Let's see. It's dated February twenty-sixth. The letter doesn't say where it came from, but the report notes that the postmark shows it was mailed in Miami, Florida, on the twenty-seventh."

"Miami! That's a long way from Fuldenville." It couldn't have been Snuffy, then.

"I've thought of that. If he'd been here on the twenty-fourth, as he says in the letter—but here—let me read it. The Department writes, as of March first, 'The following communication was received today. It would seem to require immediate investigation . . .' They go on with some details of procedure and what not. Here's the letter itself. 'Dear Sir: I had business at the farm of a man named Zertic at Fuldenville, near the old Bannerton race track, on the twenty-fourth. They had a sick horse there which they were trying to hide. I saw the horse by accident and I am sure he had glanders. I have seen a case before and it looked just like the other one. Sores all over and running from the nose. I think they must have killed the horse that night because I heard a shot and I could not locate him in the morning before I left. I saw tracks where it looked like he'd been drug away into a field.'" Dr. Parkie interrupted himself enthusiastically. "That certainly bears out what you found, doesn't it!"

"It does, all right. Did you look for the horse?"

"Well, no. My first concern was for the rest of the stock, of course. I quarantined the place and did the mallein test on every horse in sight. All negative. The Zertics are pretty belligerent—"

"You can say that again."

"Yes, you certainly discovered it! They claimed I'd ruined their reputation and that nobody'd dare buy a horse from them for months. There's something in that, you know."

"Of course."

"So, from what you've told me tonight, they waited until they thought it was all over to dig out the carcass and burn it. That's quite a job—if you've ever tried it."

"From what I saw, I can believe that. Let's hear the rest of the letter."

"That's all there is. It concludes by saying, 'These people will not report to you as they should do. I thought I better tell you about it.' It is signed, 'Yours truly, John Foster.'"

Before I let Eddie go home that night I'd extracted a promise from him to find a Miami John Foster who had had something to do with horses.

14

My Sunday was quiet and Katieless. I spent most of it alternating between trying to assort a lot of ideas which wouldn't assort and distributing pieces of the *Herald Tribune* around the apartment. I decided what my case needed was a little high-grade catalysis. There were a dozen violently explosive elements in the pot but they refused to have anything to do with each other. Somebody would have to chuck in a new element that would start something.

. . . And that, boys and girls, was the very night somebody did. An unnamed but co-operative individual blew the lid off the pot with a dead catalytic in the suddenly, deceased person of Joe Herrick.

The phone had rung about ten o'clock and I'd dripped my way out of the shower to find Eddie Marsh on the other end—all business.

"Doc, wasn't Joe Herrick the man you suspected was with Patsy Dahl when they jumped you?"

"Yes. I'd seen them together at the Ricky Club. Why?"

"He's dead. Shot. I want to see you right away."

"Where?"

"You might as well come up here if you can make it fast—Tenth Avenue and Fifty-fourth. You'll see the police cars."

I hurried into some clothes and beat it for a cab. We went west across Fifty-third and as we turned into Tenth Avenue I saw a crowd on the sidewalk up the block. I gave the driver a buck and slipped out before we got to the cops. One of Eddie's men was in the doorway of a building. He said, "Hiya, Doc. Upstairs. Second floor."

I ran up the stairs. There was an open door on the right. Eddie called to the man in the hall to let me in. The experts were all over the place—a decent-looking two-room apartment.

"Hello, Doc. I didn't think much of *your* murder. Come in and see how you like *mine*."

"You got a corpse?"

"Sure. In the bedroom. I don't let mine get buried until I find them." Eddie waved me into the room. Joe Herrick's body was loosely hung off the edge of the bed, his right arm dangling to the floor. He had been shot directly in the right ear.

"Would he have had enough left to crawl into that position, Doc?"

"That depends on what you find inside. He *could* have gone out and bought a coffin for himself. Brain wounds are very tricky, sometimes."

Eddie shrugged. "Sometimes I think you're not quite delicate."

"Wait till you dig up Goddard."

"Leave Goddard out of this. You're just trying to get him into the act."

"He'll be in the act before you take any bows on it, I'll tell you that, my friend."

"What makes you so sure?"

"Patsy Dahl and Joe Herrick had something on somebody—together. Before *they* had it, *Goddard* had it. Goddard talked too much in front of Dahl's girl. Goddard got himself dead. That leaves Dahl, his girl, and Herrick. Herrick has now got himself dead. That leaves it cozy." I was pleased with my reasoning but dreaded Eddie's next question. I tried to head it off. "Where's Dahl now?"

"In Fifty-fourth Street station—cooling his heels. Okey, chum, what did they have on whom?"

"That's for all the refrigerators and the trip to Bermuda, but I'll get the answer. You go right ahead liking your murder and I'll keep on liking mine. I'll toss you the solution to this one as a by-product—like Mama used to let you lick the bowl when she frosted a cake."

"That has a bitter and familiar sound." Marsh shook his head. "It can't be that way again, Doc! I won't have it. Why the hell don't you just go home again and pretend I never called you? Then I'll trot over to Dahl's room, like any other cop, and find the right gun."

"So why did you call me in the first place?"

"I think I've forgotten. I should have known better, anyway."

"Okey, chum. If I can guess Dahl, you won't find anything. Go and listen to his alibi and then play it smart and turn him loose for a while. On your way home, bring your little black notebook to my place. I'll give you all the right names—and, what's more, pretty close to the right order."

Raschel, one of Eddie's guys, came in and said the wagon was outside and could they have the body. The lieutenant kicked a flashbulb across the floor. "Yeah. We're through here." We walked down the stairs and passed the basket coming in.

Marsh said, "Want to come along while I talk to Dahl?"

I thought it over. There wouldn't be anything to gain and there could be a lot to lose by turning up with the police. I could always talk to Dahl. "I'll pass it up. When we talk to him next time, we'll have something to say."

Eddie ran me home without conversation. As he let me out he said, "Unless I run into something, very direct, Doc, I'm going to play this thing your way—treat it as though I'd never heard of any trouble at the Ricky Club."

"I would."

Marsh grinned. "That doesn't reassure me much, kid, but I'll take a chance." He gunned the motor. "Well, here we go again!"

I watched the police car roll down the street, wondering, as I had wondered so often, how anybody could worry about a police state in this country while we had cops like Eddie Marsh.

Shortly before midnight he called and asked if I was still up. Shortly afterward he hove in, looking tired.

"What's with Dahl?" I could tell by his attitude it hadn't been much.

"Just as you said. An alibi. It'll take some checking to see if it's any good. He's a smart cooky. By the time I got there he had an attorney waiting for me. Neat trick—especially when he hadn't even asked to use the phone."

"What's his alibi?"

"A cutie. Neither too bad nor too good. He was having his picture taken."

"No!"

Eddie laughed. "I haven't located the photographer, but he's well enough known around—name's Edel."

"How about the time of death?"

"Loose. There are only four apartments in the building and the people were all out. One couple runs a delicatessen that stays open Sunday evenings. The others were just out on their own. Doc Gregg says eight o'clock—give or take ten minutes or so."

"Who reported it?"

"A man named Scott who lives below Herrick. They play gin rummy a good deal and Scott went up to see if he could get a game. The door was open and Herrick's hat was on the couch, so he walked in."

"What time was this?"

"Scott called us at eight fifty-six. Doc saw him around nine-thirty. At exactly eight, according to Dahl, he was waiting for the photographer fourteen blocks away. He'd made an appointment and Edel always works until ten Sunday evenings. That's in the phone book. It's close."

"Maybe you can get Gregg to squidge a little on the earlier side. Otherwise you'll have a hell of a time breaking that one for a jury."

"The trouble is that Gregg's opinion slants toward the later side. He says it's more likely to be after eight than before. You're right about the jury business, though. Unless I get a lot more it'll never get to a jury."

"That's why you're here. To get a lot more. Haul out the book and write down some ideas."

"Never mind the book. I'm careful what I write in it. Haul out your ideas first." Eddie took his coat off and hung it on the back of a chair while I hunted up the cigarettes and an ash tray. We settled down and didn't say anything for a minute. I was organizing my thoughts.

Eddie said, "Once upon a time . . ."

"Why not? Once upon a time, a New Orleans gambler approached the owner of a pretty well-known restaurant with an idea of joining forces. They made quite a lot of money and the gambler got the big-league fever. By that time he owned half the restaurant. He wanted to close up and come to New York. He wanted, also, to drop the back-room gambling and bet the works on a big-town nitery. His partner objected but came along, retaining only a small interest in the business, to act as headwaiter."

"Lauziere."

"Lauziere. Also a smart cooky if my guess is any good. They make dough all over the place for several weeks after the opening and the gambler, Fogan, gets most of it. He's a personable guy and cuts a pretty handsome figure around the café caballeros. He gets respectable and smug. He treats Lauziere not too well. Meantime, Lauziere rescues a very good-looking torch singer from the minors and spends some of his saved-up dough having her coached. He books her into the joint and the now respectable Fogan falls for her. She persuades him to buy some running horses, which he does, including one good-quality stakes-winning filly which is apparently the pride of his life. The torch singer has, with this, accomplished more than meets the eye."

"How come, Scheherazade?"

"With the wisdom of a woman, O Sultan, she got nice jobs for her former suitor, a trainer of race horses, and for her father, a rubber of same. So far, very pleasant. However, there arrives at the back door of the club on the same day the filly is unloaded at the track a little man known as Snuffy. He washes dishes, talks too much about horses and other mysteries and, finally, goes away and dies of glanders."

"You think."

"I think. I stand corrected. Will you have a drink?"

"I'll take a rain check. Get on with the yarn."

"From the time the little man died, everybody in the place, including two random customers by the names of Dahl and Herrick, start searching his meager possessions for something."

Eddie snorted. "That would include your humanitarian visit to Snuffy's quarters, of course?"

"Quite right. It also includes the slugging of one Maggie Marra, a performer in the show. She was helping me by making a private search at the time, I'm sorry to say. Whoever hit her got away with Goddard's old suitcase and whatever it contained."

Eddie finally hauled out his black book. "So, if Joe Herrick got it, he hasn't got it any more."

"Magnificent deduction! I'll top that with another gem. If Herrick got it, whoever killed him's got it now."

"You're amazing! You leave me nothing to do. I only have to find out who did all this and what he did it for."

"That's right. Now, just to clarify your mind further, write these neat facts in your little book. Fogan dislikes and distrusts Lauziere, and, incidentally, knows he was at the track the night the mare was killed. Lauziere hates Fogan completely and cordially. He's planning to get the business back—all of it—when he can put the squeeze on Fogan, who is about broke."

"The hell he is!"

"He's over his head and needs capital to stay in business. Lauziere's got all his New Orleans sockful ready. Rita, undoubtedly influenced by Lauziere, has changed her attitude completely toward Fogan—dislikes him, in fact. Seems very bitter about it. Tom Bradford is in love with Rita and hates Fogan and Lauziere both. Also, Tom is broke and has to stay in Fogan's employ and good graces."

"Where do Dahl and Herrick come in?"

"Dahl's a wise guy. He's a well-heeled vagrant always looking for a fast dollar. Herrick was a stooge—strictly. Suppose Dahl got wind of a piece of scandal of some kind and confirmed it by his girl's reports on Snuffy—who'd arrived at the back door to peddle the scandal for peanuts . . ."

"So he knocks Snuffy off and takes over the deal himself."

"Something like that, but there's a terrific flaw in the idea that Dahl killed Goddard. Snuffy, although he didn't die for ten days or so, was actually murdered about February twenty-fourth or -fifth—probably at Fuldenville. Dahl would have had to be sure of his information before that, I think, or he'd never have let him get near a glanderous horse. Remember, Dahl was still looking for something after Goddard died."

"I've got too much to remember now." Eddie closed his book and got up. "All I can say to you is not to get so damned smart this time. I'm getting too old to go leaping around dodging gunfire to furnish that old corn for your last chapters."

I made some crack about yesterday's corn being tomorrow's bourbon and saw him to the door. Eddie hadn't been kidding about the gunfire I'd brought on by getting in over my head. I saw that the doors were locked before I went to bed that night.

Patsy Dahl thought I knew a lot more about his business than I did and nothing is more irritating to the middle ear than a bullet.

15

The clinic took over on Monday morning and I labored diligently until after one o'clock, when I pushed the buzzer for what turned out to be the last time. Tom Bradford walked into the office. He was all dressed up in a blue suit.

"Hello, Tom. How long have you been out there? Why didn't you holler?"

"I'm in no hurry, Doc. I've got nowhere to go." The guy slumped down at my desk and looked like he had troubles. He didn't smell of horse. I asked him what was on his mind.

"I'm out of business."

"The hell you are! Fogan?"

"In person. He turned up early this morning and told me to deliver his horses to Harry Knapp. He's sold out."

"Who'd he sell to?"

"He didn't say." Tom looked around for a place to put his hat. I took it away from him and chucked it on the desk, "He didn't say much of anything—just that he was sorry but he'd had to sell his horses and I could continue to bill him until May fifteenth."

"You still have a few others, haven't you?"

"Three and my lead pony. I called the owners and they agreed to let Knapp have them too. He runs a public stable, you know. I even sold the pony to him. That cleans me out."

"What are you planning to do?" I needn't have asked. The man was pretty bewildered.

"Hell, Doc. I'm a horse trainer! How can you plan things to do if you haven't got any horses?" He gave me a punchy grin. "I'll probably get a job rubbing 'em. I ain't proud."

"Are you that broke?"

"Just about. Fogan's fees up to the fifteenth of May will get me out with the feed man. I owe the bank some money down home—maybe I can stall that for a couple of months."

"How about right now, Tom?"

"Harry Knapp gave me three-fifty for the pony. I'll get along. If you had the idea I came here to borrow money, forget it." He ruffled his feathers some.

"I didn't think you did." I offered him a cigarette and we smoked a little while with nothing much to say. I broke it up, finally. "Maybe it's just as well, Tom."

"What do you mean?"

"Beside the fact that Fogan needs dough . . ."

"Fogan needs dough?"

"Badly—in large chunks. The club is running behind and has to be refinanced."

"So that's why he sold out."

"Maybe so—maybe not. It wouldn't get him the kind of money he needs, for one thing. More importantly, somebody in that group is putting the bite on him. I think it's blackmail."

"Do you suppose it could have anything to do with Rita?" Bradford took on a quick sunburn. When I asked if he had any special reason for suggesting it, his brown face went brickish.

"She called me this morning."

"Oh? About Fogan's selling his string?"

"Yes." He shook his head like a colt with hay on its ears. "She's quitting her job."

"I don't know why I hadn't expected that, Tom. She give any reason?"

"Only that she's afraid of, as she put it, 'what might happen at the club.' No more than that."

"What did Rita say about Fogan's getting out of racing?"

"That what Fogan did was his own business but that I was well out of any connection with him."

"No more?"

"No. She said she'd tell me sometime." Tom looked very directly into my face for a wavering moment. "Rita's coming to see you, Doc. If she's in some kind of a jam, help her, will you?"

"Of course I will. Count on it."

"Thanks." Bradford got up and took his hat. "That's why I came. I don't give a damn about what those people do to me but I don't want them to do anything to her." He stuck out his hand in an embarrassed way. We shook. He turned to go—swung back. "As long as Rita's out of it, you better forget the promise you made me about investigating the filly's death. You can jail the bunch of them as far as I'm concerned."

After Tom had left, I emptied ash trays and straightened things up a bit. Rita could, possibly, put a lot of loose ends together for me once she'd quit the club. She telephoned about three-thirty and arrived shortly afterward, giving with contralto amenities and accepting an old-fashioned. Once prettily settled, she led off.

"I need some advice, Doctor."

"Sore throat?"

She smiled. "Recurrent headaches. I've begun to think they're an occupational disease."

"Maybe you're allergic to somebody." I was content to play games until she settled down.

"It isn't house dust. Listen, Doc. My father told me that Phil Lauziere deliberately killed Rick Fogan's filly."

"When did he tell you that?"

"Last night. I've been helping him a little, and when he came by for his check last evening he told me Rick was selling out before Lauziere burned the barn down." Rita poked at her old-fashioned. "I didn't believe him until he said he'd seen Phil at the track that night."

"Fogan knows Lauziere was there. I told him."

". . . and Dad told you?"

"That's right." I put down my glass. "Rita, you said you needed my advice. I'm sure you can use some. Tom tells me you've quit your job. He was here a couple of hours ago."

"Tom was?" She stuck her nose up. "I wish he'd let me tend to my own affairs!"

"Do you make a point of leading with that determined chin of yours?"

"Have I led with my chin?"

"I think you have. You wouldn't be asking my advice if you'd managed your own affairs better."

She could still laugh a little at herself. "I guess you're right. I'm certainly in the middle of something very unpleasant. Apparently I've been helping Phil Lauziere in some sort of a conspiracy against Rick. It frightens me."

"It should. Tell me how you figure it. From the beginning."

"Lord, Doc! I can't tell, now, when the beginning was." She frowned as she thought it over. "Maybe it started about two weeks ago—or three. The little man they called Snuffy was working in the kitchen . . ."

I did some arithmetic. "Three weeks, then. Snuffy's been dead more than two."

"It was a few days before he disappeared. Lauziere came to me and said he'd seen the man closeted with Fogan in the office. Phil seemed very much disturbed."

"He could well have been." Pay dirt ahead!

"I see that, now." She fussed around with her bag. "I don't know how I could have been so damned dumb."

I looked at her alert, intelligent eyes and rejected the idea that she'd gotten herself into trouble by being dumb. It's more characteristic of the breed to get themselves out of trouble by being dumb. I uttered some platitude about all of us and she went on.

"Phil warned me not to say anything about it and not to join in any gossip around the club. He said he knew who the dishwasher was and that he probably would try to make trouble."

"What sort of trouble?"

"Lauziere wouldn't tell me—and never did. After the man disappeared, Phil said nothing about it whatever, but a few days later he hid an old suitcase and some other stuff in my dressing room and made me promise to forget they were there. Then things began to happen. Fogan and Lauziere had a tremendous row, as a starter."

"Did you know what it was about?"

"No. It could have been about me. Fogan was being—over-attentive and Phil didn't like it."

I avoided asking her if the headwaiter was also being—over-attentive. "Then what?"

"Then the filly died and you turned up. You'll remember that I saw Patsy Dahl prowling in Rick's office that night."

". . . adding to your suspicion that something was wrong."

"I'll get to that later." She lit a cigarette. "When it came out in the papers about your being attacked, I knew it was Snuffy—"

"How?"

"Phil had mentioned his last name—I think inadvertently. Then, when I came in to dress last night, the suitcase was gone and there was blood spattered on my dressing table . . . what are you laughing at?"

"Nothing very funny. I'll tell you later. Go on with the story."

"I was scared and went out to tell somebody about it. I couldn't find Phil and when I went to Rick's office he'd been talking to a man I'd seen around with Dahl."

I was taught not to holler at ladies, but I hollered then! "Joe Herrick? A big, dumb-looking guy with a bent nose?"

"Yes. That describes him. I didn't know who he was."

"What time was this?"

"Probably seven-fifteen or so. The dinner show is eight-fifteen."

"Rick knows you saw him with Herrick?"

"Absolutely not. I went to the door and heard Fogan and some man talking in low tones, so I walked back down the hall and waited until the man went out. When I saw who it was—and remembered Patsy Dahl's searching or whatever he did in the office—I got more suspicious and scared. I decided not to tell anybody."

"Has Lauziere said anything about the stuff being gone?"

"Not a word. He may not even know it's no longer there."

"I think he does. Look, Rita, are you sure you've told me everything that Lauziere—or Fogan, for that matter—has said to you? Anything that could have any bearing on people like Snuffy or Dahl or each other?"

"Quite sure. Is there any reason for you to think I haven't?"

"If there is, it's pretty vague. I'll tell you, perfectly frankly, that I don't know whether it refers to you or not. Snuffy, apparently, blamed a woman for his troubles. I was wondering if it could have been somebody around the club."

"It would seem strange. He was old and—rather unpleasant the few times I saw him. Some of the girls hung around and gossiped with him, I understand. Mrs. Marra . . ." She left it hanging bitterly and brushed Maggie off her skirt.

"Goddard, when he was dying, said something like, 'It's on her account. It's on her account.'" To avoid discussion of Snuffy's disease, I changed the subject. "How about Tom Bradford?"

She picked me up quickly. "Why do you include Tom, Doc?"

"Because, as much as I like him, I can't leave him out. Tom was under some obligations to Fogan as his trainer and under some rather more realistic obligations to others. Incidentally, he also feels a considerable responsibility for you—for some reason or other."

Rita's blush was more attractive, if less comprehensive, than Bradford's as she changed the subject. "Perhaps you can see how I felt when Dad told me what he did last night."

"You don't seem to have read the papers this morning."

"I haven't. Why?"

"Joe Herrick—the man you saw talking to Fogan—was shot and killed last night."

She sat stiff and said nothing but a low "Oh!"

"Perhaps you see, now, why it's so important that you tell me all you know about the situation at the club."

"Because I know too much about some things and not enough about others? Could I be in any danger, Doc?"

"I don't know who might be in danger and who might not. Somebody is bound to be. There are too many people concerned.

I'm not in too pretty a spot, myself." I slid the ash tray closer to her and she ground out her cigarette. "Have you told me the whole business?"

"Everything."

"That's that, then. Thanks. I'm glad you've quit. You're not going back tonight, are you?"

"No. There's a girl who's taken over for me a number of times. I reported ill and called her." She smiled. "Maggie Marra will set the show. Poor Maggie!"

"What's the matter with Maggie?"

"Her husband beats her." Rita got up and put her bag under her arm. I left Danny Marra in his wife-beating status and walked to the door with her. "Thanks, Doc. I hope I've helped. Both Phil and Rick seemed so perturbed when you turned up that I suspected you might be trying to find something out."

"I was—and am. With the full knowledge, by the way, of everybody concerned."

"They may know about it, but they don't like it. Naturally I'd rather you didn't say anything about what I've told you." She started putting on her gloves. "I'm afraid they'll make a fuss over my quitting."

"Stay ill for a little while. I have a hunch a week will do." If Snuffy Goddard was to bear witness as to the cause of his murder, he'd have to get at it pretty soon. "Tell me, Rita, when you discovered the suitcase was gone, did you notice anything else under your dressing table?"

She gave me a quick, sideways look and laughed. "I didn't tell you they'd been hidden under my dressing table."

Dumb? Not this one. "It seemed like the best place to hide them."

"All right, Doc. Was it your blood I found spattered around?"

"It belonged to an acquaintance of mine. There's a laugh in it for you sometime—not right now. So what about it? Did you find anything?"

"Nothing you wouldn't expect. Some old junk of mine that had been kicked under there and a paper bag with some former singer's atomizer in it."

I'm afraid I yelled at the lady again. "An *atomizer!*"

"Why not? You've been around show business long enough to . . ."

"Where is it now? What did you do with it?"

"I threw it in my wastebasket. Where's the fire?"

"I'm going with you. To the club. You're still ill if there's anyone around—just getting something. I suppose it's in the trash cans by this time."

"I don't know what this is all about, but it isn't in the trash. The cleaning women are off on Sunday nights. The waiters take care of the big room but that's all."

I grabbed my coat and hat and we hurried out. The club was deserted except for the kitchen help and an electrician setting lights. When I got home, I sat for a long time studying the People's Exhibit A.

16

The atomizer had been wiped clean and undoubtedly refilled with what looked and, from a respectful distance, smelled like one of the usual proprietary oil-base nose drops. I felt certain it had once contained beef broth, similar in color, and scrapings of glanderous excretion from the nose or skin of the horse. You can't grow—or even maintain—a culture of *Bacilli mallei* in mineral oil, eucalyptus, and ephedrin. In ordinary grocery-store beef soup, however, you stand a good chance of keeping a thriving colony.

Bacteriologist? Hell, no! Opportunist. Who'd try to carry germs in a solution advertised to kill them? Beef broth is probably the best known of all culture media and, if the killer didn't know about it, the encyclopedia or a veterinary handbook would tell him. I wondered if there were a library in Bannerton.

A telephone call from Eddie Marsh woke me up in the morning.

"I guess we can start on your Ricky Club people, Doc. I turned Dahl loose last night. I can't hold him on what we've got."

"Made his alibi stand up, did he?"

"Within six or seven minutes. It's good enough to keep him out of jail, even as a material witness—so far."

"So you're back to my murder now?"

"I'm back to the mess you stuck your nose into, at least. Miami reported on your John Foster this morning, by the way."

"Good. What about him?"

"There are three of 'em. The one you want owns a horse van."

"That's my man! How can I reach him?"

"Got your pencil?" Eddie said something over his shoulder. "Hold it a minute, Doc, here's more on him." Some fumbling around. "They're thorough down there. I suggested Foster might have been North recently and here's the answer. I'll read it: 'John Foster delivered race horse to Martin Zertic, Fuldenville, February twenty-fourth, from Palmetto Park fairgrounds. Returned next day, empty, arriving Miami twenty-seventh.' That's the teletype. You can reach Foster care of Mainland & Keys Trucking Service—5 8, 6639. That do you?"

"Fits like a watch stem. Foster vanned the filly to Fuldenville and Goddard brought her to New York."

"What makes you think so?" Marsh grinned over the phone. He can do that. "You haven't placed Goddard in Fuldenville yet."

"The hell I haven't! If you don't like it, get your boys to find me another glanderous horse. He was there, all right, and he turned up in New York the day the filly was delivered."

"Bradford should be able to identify Goddard, then."

"Good Lord! I hadn't thought of that. He should at least remember what the guy looked like. He won't look like that when you dig him up."

"*Quiet!* Listen, Doc, I want to talk to those people up at the Ricky Club. I can't figure out any connection with Herrick, but you seem to think there is one. Who shall I start on?"

"Fogan." I told Eddie of Rick's talk with Herrick the evening of the shooting.

"You been holding out on me again?"

"No. I just learned it."

"Hell! He's the guy I've been looking for! I haven't been able to find anybody that had seen Herrick since early Sunday morning. Want to come along?"

"This time, yes. I've got some ideas about the spot Fogan's been in and I think I can head off a lot of doubletalk."

"I'll pick you up in ten minutes."

"Not so fast. Give the guy a break! He works till after three. It's only nine-thirty. Telephone him at noon and make a date."

"Okey. I'll let you know."

After Eddie had hung up, I put in a call for John Foster. He wasn't around but was expected before noon. I had the operator leave a number and fixed some browned corned beef hash and coffee. I was washing the dishes when the call came through. I told Foster who I was and that I was on the trail of a case of glanders in a human.

"That's awful bad, isn't it, Doc?"

"Yes. The man's dead. We can't identify him fully. I wondered if you might remember him being at Fuldenville. He was a small man—jockey-size—and close to sixty. Could have been called Snuffy or Pat, Paddy or Goddard."

"Nobody like that around there the night I was at the place. At least not while I was awake. I slept in my van and got away at a little after daylight."

"You reported you heard a shot that night?"

"Yeah. I don't know just when. It might have been real late. I was parked pretty well away from the barn toward the road. There was people movin' around and I heard an engine runnin' some. I thought, afterward, it might have been the tractor when they hauled the dead horse off."

"Somebody could have come in with a truck, then, and you might not have known it?"

"That's right. Your man could've been there during the night but I never seen him."

"Was the horse you delivered still there in the morning?"

"I don't know, Doc, they put her on the far side of the house in some sort of shed. It looked like it had been for cows once because they bedded her down in what seemed to be an old bull pen."

"That wasn't where you found the glanderous horse?"

"No. That's why I got curious. There was a big horse barn right where I pulled up and it was empty. While they was putting up the mare I looked around in there and found the horse with glanders."

"But they'd tried to keep it out of sight?"

"Yeah. Not only in the last stall down in the dark end, but they'd tacked up feed sacks across the side of the box. That's how I figured they wasn't going to report it."

"Okey, John, that's swell. Tell me; was the name of the mare you hauled Armada? A three-year-old thoroughbred?"

"That's right. I brought the papers and all along. She come from Palmetto Park where she's been boardin' all winter. Charley Presky had her."

"Did Presky work her?"

"She galloped light all the time. Charley said she was fit to ship but hadn't done no fast work. Presky don't train running horses. Maybe you didn't know. Palmetto is a state park where they got a big hotel an' ridin' horses. They's a fairgrounds there but they haven't used it for years."

"So, as far as you know, Presky doesn't have anything to do with racing."

"That's right, Doc."

"Thanks a lot. Who signed for her, by the way?"

"One of the two big guys there at the farm. Martin Zertic, was it?"

"Probably. He's the boss. I may want to call you again if you don't mind."

"Call me any time, Doc, so long."

That put Snuffy there during the night of February twenty-fourth. The horse must have been buried sometime before daylight. Armada was delivered in New York the next day. Nobody would be able to tell me who had been with Goddard that night but my little playmates, the Zertics. Next time I interviewed those energetic characters, I'd be prepared.

Eddie called me about one-thirty and said how about it. His date with Rick Fogan was for two o'clock—at the club. I got some clothes on and wondered how to treat Fogan. Eddie had enough connection established between the Dahl-Herrick team and the club to handle it entirely out of his own book. I wanted information from Fogan but it didn't make sense to try to get it in front of Eddie.

On the way up, I suggested that the lieutenant keep the interview strictly within the limits of his own knowledge—concealing his sources, of course, for the meeting Herrick had had with Fogan.

There was a bare working light, in the lobby and a man was sweeping. Eddie walked up to him. "Where will I find Mr. Fogan? I've got an appointment with him."

"You Mr. Marsh?"

"That's right."

"Back in the office. He said you was coming."

Eddie took off down the long hall and we found Fogan's door open.

"Come in, Lieutenant, how do you do?" Then he saw me. "Well, Doc, you joined the force?"

"The force's joined me, Rick. I've got a little grudge to settle with the lad that conked me."

". . . and who was that?"

"Patsy Dahl." Rick gave me a curious look and came up with a small smile.

"I begin to see the light. Sit down, gentlemen."

Marsh said, "I don't begin to see any at all. You know this Dahl, Mr. Fogan?" He used the honest, puzzled manner with which he robs newcomers at poker.

"Yes. I know him—as a customer. He runs around with one of the girls in the show and comes in pretty often." The quiet, gray eyes turned to the big cop. "I understand his partner was killed Sunday night. I suppose that's why you're interested, Lieutenant Marsh?"

"That's exactly why I'm interested. You say 'his partner'—do you know what the man did for a living?"

Rick smiled. "I haven't the slightest idea. I'd be somewhat surprised if he did anything. I spoke of Herrick as his partner because they're always around together."

"I see." Eddie accepted a cigarette from Fogan. "Thanks. I'm trying to put them together on Sunday night, but I can't. You didn't happen to see Dahl anyplace that night, did you, Mr. Fogan?"

"No. I was around all evening and he didn't come in."

". . . or Herrick?"

Rick responded with a punchy grin. "I'm glad you attended the party, Doc, I need your help right now, I'm afraid."

"I think maybe I see why." I tried to be very gentle about it. "Is it because you hesitate to bring some of the—minor unpleasantnesses to light?"

"Precisely; I feel that it's important to give the lieutenant certain facts, but dislike to go into some phases which are not police matters."

"I'm sure Lieutenant Marsh will understand. I have suggested to him that you were being made the object of considerable personal malice. Eddie is interested in finding out who killed Herrick—not who's been playing dirty tricks on you."

Marsh spoke up. "I'm afraid I'll have to be the judge of what's pertinent and what isn't, but I've sifted a whole lot of personal troubles out of murder cases in my time. You're bound to run into them when people are under penetrative investigation."

"Thank you for your reassurance, Lieutenant." Fogan folded his long hands on the desk. "Joe Herrick came to this office Sunday evening to see me."

Marsh played it very straight. "That could be important to us. Did you ask him here?"

"Most emphatically not. If I'd had any choice in the matter I'd never have admitted either Dahl or Herrick to the club at any time. He came unannounced."

"What time was this?"

"Shortly after seven. He stayed only a few minutes."

The black notebook was out at this point. "Mind telling me what he wanted?"

Rick smiled. "No. . . . You see, Marsh, that's the personal part of it. He wanted to peddle some information."

I alerted at once. Eddie said, "I have to ask you what sort of information. It apparently was something that somebody didn't want him to peddle. He walked out of here and somebody shot him."

"It was—although killing him seems a pretty drastic method of keeping him from exposing a person who had committed no real crime. A little over a week ago a racing filly of mine was poisoned—killed. Because, as Doc has told you, I am being made the victim of some—shall we say jealous attacks. I did not report it to the police. That is my privilege in such a matter, I believe."

"I think it would be." Eddie leaned forward toward Fogan. "So Herrick offered to sell out the person who killed your horse?"

"That's right."

"Did you take him up?"

"No."

"Why?"

"Because I know who killed the mare."

"Is that what you told Herrick?"

"No. I told him nothing but to get out and stay out."

"So a couple of hours later, Herrick is dead." Eddie did a little smiling of his own—for the first time. "I'd be remiss in my duty, Fogan, if I didn't ask you how you spent Sunday evening—from the time Hetrick left until, say, ten o'clock."

"Of course you would. I spent Sunday evening as I spend almost every Sunday evening. It's a good night in the club as a rule and I make a point of being on the job."

"You were here constantly during that period, then?" Eddie didn't look up from writing in his book. "Where you were seen at frequent intervals?"

"I haven't given it any thought. I know I was busy—I remember that most distinctly. When I'm busy, people see me. Yes, I think my alibi will hold."

We said pleasant things and left. As we were pulling away from the curb Eddie said, "What time does this Lauziere get around?"

"I was here as early as five-thirty one night and he was on the job. He'll give you caviar and cocktails in his office if you call on him at that hour. They're good, too."

"I stand a fair chance of landing back on a beat every time I get tangled up with you. All I need now is cocktails and caviar." Marsh beetle-browed across Broadway and turned left. "Fogan's right enough about the personal thing. I don't give a damn about Lauziere's killing the horse—though it's my idea of the bottom in low tricks. All I want to know is where the Frenchman was on Sunday night."

We both thought for another couple of blocks. I finally made up my mind what I wanted to find out—if not why.

"You know what, Eddie?"

"What?"

"That's just backwards for me. I don't think I give a damn where Lauziere was Sunday night. I'd like to know why he killed the filly."

17

As I stepped out of the elevator at my floor, somebody said, "I want to see you, Doc." It was very low and very tough. The man was sitting against the window sill at the end of the hall. I couldn't see his face against the light, but it had to be Patsy Dahl.

"Okey, Patsy, come on in." I unlocked the door and waited for Dahl to walk ahead of me. "Sit down."

He said nothing, but stood in the middle of the living room with his hat on. He was nervous and mean. I took off my coat and hat and tossed them on the table. "What's on your mind?"

"Cops."

"I understand you've been talking with them lately."

"Don't get cute. I'm not having any." The guy contrived to make himself sound more unpleasant than usual. "This is business."

"All right, Dahl, so it's business. What about the cops?"

"Why'd you take Eddie Marsh to the Ricky Club today?"

"I didn't take him. He took me."

"Why?"

"Marsh is collecting alibis for the time Joe Herrick was killed. Didn't he get one from you?"

Dahl overlooked the crack and got back to the subject. "What have the people at the club got to do with Herrick's death?"

"You're asking me?"

"What's that mean?"

"It means that if you don't know I certainly don't." I began to feel a little tough, myself. I figured this guy was in no spot to be pushing me around. "Last time I saw you, Dahl, you were all for making some kind of a deal with me—you'd cut yourself in. Remember?"

"You're damned right I cut myself in!"

"Okey. You're in. What's more, you're in it all alone, chum—just you and little Eve Tillory." He looked less tough and more puzzled. I laid it on. "Now that Joe's out."

"What about you?"

"I never was in, Dahl—and if I had been I'd have had sense enough to be out by now."

"What's the matter with it?"

"The main difficulty seems to be that everybody that knows anything about it gets killed." I decided to blow the works. "If you shot Herrick, you—"

"I didn't shoot Herrick and the cops know it. I wasn't anywhere near the place."

". . . and you've got the proofs to prove it. How did they turn out?"

Dahl made an angry gesture with his hand. "You sure get your nose into a lot of things that are none of your business, Connor." He unbuttoned his coat and let it fall open—so I'd catch the brown of his shoulder holster. It made me sore.

"You trying to scare me, Patsy?"

"Hell, no! You're scared already."

"Not of you, chum—nor that empty holster."

He looked like he was going for it for an instant, then held up. I probably shouldn't have said it, but I would have laid five to two he had more sense than to carry a gun with the police watching him. I found myself practically on top of him and backed off carefully. "So what am I scared of, tough guy?"

"Are you kidding? You get your hands on a chunk of real dough for once, but right in the middle of the deal you lose your guts and go running to the cops. Somebody scared you good!" He leaned back against the mantel to make it look better.

"I've got some news for you, Dahl. I tried to tell you before but you wouldn't believe it—until I came up with some wrong answers. You'd better believe it now. I never had my hands on any dough—real or otherwise—connected with what you call the deal. But I'm damned well going to find the guy who has."

The man did something with his face—sneered or snarled. It didn't pretty him up any, whatever it was. "Turned copper again, eh? Maybe you can figure out who killed Joe. I'd like to know that, myself."

"Maybe that's the person I'm after and maybe not. I'm not interested in who killed Herrick. That's Marsh's job. The guy I'm after is a lousy horse butcher."

Dahl's eyes glinted interest and he turned them off quickly. "You don't know who killed Fogan's horse?"

I thought it over a second and decided to say, "No. Do you?"

He laughed—never taking a surprised stare off me. "Of course not, Doc! How would I know a thing like that? Why, bless your little heart, I think I'm going to believe you!"

That really burned me. It also made sense and I gave up my earnest desire to beat the information out of the guy. He knew some of it, all right—enough to set me right—but he didn't know all of it, I felt, or he wouldn't have been so damned gay about the thing. I made up my mind to lay my ideas on the line.

"Listen, Dahl! Did it ever occur to you that everybody who has known as much about this matter as you do has been taken suddenly dead?"

"Like who?"

"Oh . . . like Joe Herrick"

"You're nuts! Joe didn't know enough about what was going on to be worth anything to anybody."

"That's what you think."

Dahl frowned. "That's what I know. Somebody might have *thought* he knew—but he didn't."

"Herrick thought he had something that was worth while to somebody."

He jerked his arm off the mantel and took a step toward me. "What do you mean by that?"

"Now maybe, for once, I tell you a few facts you don't already know. You'll love this! Shortly after seven o'clock on Sunday evening your loyal friend Joe was trying to peddle everything he knew to Rick Fogan."

That did it. Dahl lost his bravado, but quick. He started a couple of remarks that didn't make it before he got one out.

"Did Fogan tell you that?"

My turn, now, and I rode the guy. "How do you like it, Patsy? You think you're such a wise guy and your sidekick is up there selling you out to Fogan—making a sucker out of you!"

"Goddammit! I asked you if Fogan told you."

"He told Eddie Marsh." I took a chance and sat down on the couch. "It didn't help the police to nest on your alibi, I can tell you that."

He sleepwalked across the room and stood in front of me. Just stood there looking at me. I said, "Sit down, Patsy. I've got a couple more things to say I think you ought to hear."

He sat down—cautiously—as though he suspected a tack. "All right, let's have it."

"You say you didn't kill Joe Herrick—"

"I told you I—"

"Hold it! Think, don't holler. So you didn't kill Herrick. It's a fair guess that somebody did—and now you know the reason why."

"It don't make sense."

"I think it makes better sense to you than it does to me, Dahl, but let that go. I'll give it to you straight. I think your 'deal'—as you call it—has misfired. If you can get clean with the law, you'd better do it."

"I'm clean with the law now. What do you mean, misfired?" Defensive again.

"I mean that what started out to be a neat little plan for running Fogan out of town blew up in somebody's face. I know pretty well who dreamt it up, but I don't know who he got to carry it out for him. He wasn't in a position to do it himself. From the time—"

"Listen, Doc, nobody—"

"*You* listen. This is right on the line, Dahl. From the time the idea was cooked up, things started to go wrong with it. One man was seen talking to Rick Fogan. He's dead. Sunday night another man was seen talking to Fogan—on the same subject. He's dead. Maybe you catch on now."

I waited for him to ask me who the first dead man had been. He didn't. Instead he said, "Fogan must've killed Joe." But his heart wasn't in it.

"He's got as good an alibi as yours."

"I don't like that crack."

"It's simply a fact. If you didn't have anything to do with Herrick's death you've got nothing to worry about—from the police. But I wouldn't let that stop me worrying if I were you."

"All right—give me something to worry about."

"Sure, Patsy, glad to help in any way I can. Think this over. If you are one of the people who know too much about Snuffy Goddard's activities before he died—and I think you are—you'd better stay out of alleys and lock your door at night."

It wasn't smart to say that. Dahl looked cornered and mean. We both got up in pretty much of a hurry. I could see the guy fighting himself and thought of my .38 in the desk drawer. Then it was all over. He chewed off his farewell.

"Something tells me you'd better stay out of alleys yourself, Doc." He walked, stiff-legged, to the door. "I'll see you around."

As I watched the elevator go down, I got the feeling that maybe I'd better stay out of alleys at that. If there had ever been any question in my mind that Patsy Dahl was in serious trouble, it vanished with the green felt hat that was the last I saw of the man as he left.

The living room seemed very quiet and permanent. I sat down to figure out my next move. First, of course, Tom would have to be checked to see if Snuffy actually did arrive with the filly. So far, I'd theorized. I got Tom at home. He hadn't seen the driver because he had been in New York, talking business at the club with Fogan. Pop Asher had unloaded the horse with the help of the watchman. The van had come very late in the afternoon. I got a number where I could get Pop. The people downstairs would call him. I heard some woman howl for Mr. Asher and Pop came on.

"Why, no, Doc, come to think of it. I didn't get a good look at the feller. His truck leveled with the loading ramp all right and he just backed up and opened the doors for us from the inside. Bert Mills, the watchman, helped me?"

"Then the only time you saw him was inside the truck."

"That's right exactly, Doc. I didn't see him good even then. He was behind the mare and Bert and I was in front. By the time he was closin' the doors again, we'd got under the shed with the filly."

"Who signed for her?"

"I did. Only he was back in the seat by that time and I didn't look much at him. I signed his paper and he left."

So that was that. All I could hope to do was place Snuffy at Fuldenville, which would involve another meeting with the pugnacious Zertic brothers. I packed a small bag. My gun permit is no good outside the state of New York, but I stuck the .38 in anyway. I don't suppose Zertic had a permit to take after me with a shotgun, either. There wouldn't be any welcome on the doormat this trip.

I caught a late afternoon train to Bannerton. My pal, the local hackie, met it.

"Boy, howdy! Still sellin'?"

"This trip I'm buying. Where's the hotel?"

"Which one? There's two." He put my bag in the back seat. "Neither one of 'em worth a hoot. I'd go to the Alder if I was you—that is, unless the Zertic boys'll put you up."

I cackled with him and got in. "The Alder will do. You got a public library here?"

"A real good one, they tell me. Sets back from the street a block and a half past the hotel. I never been in it, but I guess the books are as good there as they are other places."

"Thanks." We pulled up in front of a pleasant white-painted structure. "This it?"

"That's right. Fifty cents to you, mister." I gave him six bits. "I thank you kindly, sir. Let me know, if you want to call on Marty Zertic again. He sure is interested in you!"

"How come?"

"Why say! That feller looked me up next time he come into town and ast me more questions than a schoolteacher. When I told him you left on the train, he calmed down some."

"Maybe he'll like me better this time."

"That man don't like nobody, mister. Here's a card. I couldn't find a clean one, but it reads about as good. Just gimme a call."

I told him I might, at that, and checked into the hotel. The room wasn't too bad. I stayed long enough to freshen up and walked down the street to the library. The notice in the hallway suggested politely that the customers keep silent and leave promptly at nine o'clock. A miniature old lady presided at a huge desk near the entrance.

I approached her with the understanding and dignity I usually reserve for occasions when I have to ask some fem patient to bare her hindquarters for a shot of penicillin. She apparently appreciated it. She was most cordial.

"Glanders, Doctor? I don't know quite what it is, myself. Perhaps you could give me just a *hint?"*

"It's a disease of horses and some other animals, madam."

"Oh well, now. We are a farming country around here and the Library Association is quite proud of our Agricultural Reference Section. The reference index is just on your right—Diseases, Horse, probably."

"May these books be taken out?"

"Not the ones in that file. They must be used on the premises."

"Do you keep a record of their use—as to when they are taken from the shelves?"

"Always, Dr. Connor. The staff puts them up after they're used. We ask that they be returned to this desk."

I thanked her and riffled through the card file. The Horse, Diseases of—several well-known books, some articles, and

"Glanders," Bulletin, U. S. Dept. Ag., 1934. The librarian found it for me.

"Now where would your record on the use of this bulletin be?"

She turned it over in my hand. "Right on the back. You see, there's a leaf pasted on."

I saw. There was a leaf pasted on, indeed! The last of the very few dates recorded was February twenty-fifth—the day after Zertic's animal had been destroyed.

18

There appeared to be a couple of places to eat. The busier one contained elderly waitresses in rose aprons and, undoubtedly, things like apple-and-nut salad. Mr. Mikelous' Chop House, however, did a hearty job of feeding me the sort of food a man needs to sustain him through round two of the Zertic-Connor match.

Thus reinforced, I made up my mind to inspect the pyre at the bottom of the Zertics' field. The hackie had moved from the station to a spot next to the movie.

"You want to take me to Fuldenville?"

"Get in. Marty's place?"

"The back end of it. I was interrupted the other day, you'll remember."

"I'll say you was. What're you? Detective or somethin'?"

"How good are you at minding your own business?" He was silent a second, then he said, "Good." After that he didn't say anything at all until we were almost in Fuldenville. I laughed, finally. I also had made up my mind what I was.

"You're okey, friend. I didn't mean minding your own business with me. I meant with other people."

"Oh. Good at that, too." Things got more friendly at once.

"That's fine. I'm a medical investigator."

"Somebody got the plague?"

"Somebody *had* it. He's dead."

He thought about that. I'll always like the guy. He started minding his own business right then. "What do you want me to do, mister?"

"Drive past the corner at a normal speed—then pull up behind something and let me out. Wait for me."

We stopped by a row of trees and the man turned off the lights. I got out and left the car door open. "I may have to hurry back."

"If you need any help, holler."

"What'll I holler?"

"Just holler for Ben. Name's Ben Peck."

"Thanks, Ben. If you hear me coming on the run, get your motor started, will you?"

"Leave it to me."

I walked along the shadow of the tree's to the corner and got my eyes accommodated to the dim evening light. Just as I was about to cross the road I thought I saw something moving in the field. I waited. A cigarette glowed—close to the ground—then went out. I'd seen something for sure! The dark, squat mass slowly lengthened into a man, standing. An object separated itself from the figure and in a moment I heard the ring of a shovel hitting a stray stone. One of the brothers was filling the pit and had stopped to have a smoke. He labored steadily on while I worked my way up the road to a point where I could circle around behind him. I climbed under the wire fifty yards or so below the pit and arced around. He was still shoveling when I stopped thirty feet back of him. My foot hit a fair-sized rock and I picked it up.

"Marty?" I said it right neighborly but he swung his shovel shoulder-high and whirled.

"Who the hell is that?"

I was afraid he'd yell, but he didn't. He croaked it out.

"Connor, Zertic. I want to talk to you."

He held the shovel in both hands—at port arms—and took a couple of steps toward me. "You git off this prope'ty or I'll . . ."

"Hold it right where you are, Zertic, and keep quiet. If you move or yell, I'll drop you." I neglected to name the weapon. The guy was taking no unnecessary chances, however, and halted. "Now listen to me and keep your yap shut until I get through."

"You kin talk awful tough with a gun in your hand, can't you, Connor!"

"Anybody can—provided he's got the guts and the authority to use it. I'm here on business and I'm going to make it stick, this time. If you're smart, you'll calm down and answer some questions."

"A man's got a right to bury his own horse without a lot of . . ."

"That's right, Zertic, that's *right!* I'm not interested in the horse. I'm not even interested in you. I've got no connection with the Department of Agriculture. I'm a medical investigator trying to find out why a man was murdered in New York. Now will you answer some questions for me and get it over with?"

"New York? What've we got to do with a murder in New York?"

"More than you think. Both the man that was murdered and the man that killed him were on this place during the night of February twenty-fourth."

"They couldn't 'a' been! I don't have no dealings with people like that!" The man sounded a little overwhelmed, but still challenging.

"You had dealings with this one, Zertic. You delivered a horse to him."

"February twenty-four?"

"The night you shot this horse and dragged it into the field." I waited for some response, but got none. "You did do that, didn't you, Marty? You and Jake?"

"What of it?"

"Get your mind off the damned animal! He had glanders and you didn't want your reputation spoiled. You destroyed and buried him—and had sense enough to burn the carcass after you'd read up on the disease in the Bannerton Library, next day."

"You know a lot, mister, don't you! More'n my brother and I put together. *We* didn't know if it was glanders. We just thought it could be and didn't want to take any chances. I didn't have to go to no library to look it up, either."

"The murderer did, then. I like that better anyway. All right, let's see how much more I know. A man named John Foster delivered a race mare to you on the twenty-fourth. He slept in his van and left shortly after daylight next morning. During that night you loaded the mare on another truck. The driver was a small man, close to sixty, named Snuffy—or Pat—Goddard. Listen carefully, Zertic, and come up with the right answer. Who was the man with Goddard that night?"

I could sense his sullenness, although he didn't speak.

"Who was he?" I tightened it up a little this time.

"I don't know who he was. He set in the car."

"What car? The truck?"

"No. Another car. He drove in behind the horse van as far as the edge of the barnyard. He turned off his lights and set there in the dark."

"What time was this?"

"After midnight, maybe."

". . . and you and Jake were up?"

Zertic hesitated. "Yes, we was up."

"Waiting for him?"

"No. We expected him in the morning."

I jumped on the him. "Expected *him?* Who?"

"Goddard. The man that wrote us."

"What did he write you?" I could have shaken hands with the big ape—except that I could hear him praying for one swing with that shovel.

"He wrote and said he had a horse comin' from Florida and would I put it up until he could call for it. Then, later, he wrote to expect him in the morning of February twenty-five."

"But he came during the night before and found you and Jake fixing to drag the horse off."

"He couldn't've seen the horse. We'd already drug it through the pasture gate while he was drivin' in."

"But you left the tractor on the hitch?"

"I s'pose we did."

". . . and the engine running."

"Hell! How do I know? Jake was handlin' the tractor. He might've let it idle—it's hard to start. What difference would that make?"

"Plenty, Zertic. There's something else that would make a difference. Did you stay with the man, Goddard, from the time he got off the truck until he drove away?"

"Why . . . yes. Both Jake and me. You can't accuse us of—"

"I'm not accusing you. Just tell me where Goddard went and what he did while he was on the place that night."

"When he come in with the van, Jake waved him to go on around the house to the other barn. I went along and the three of us got the mare ready an' loaded her. Mr. Goddard signed the receipt an' give me eight dollars. Then he got on the truck an' drove straight out the gate. That's all I—or anybody else—seen of him on this place."

"How long did all that take?"

"Purtineer half an hour, I s'pose. We cleaned the van bed and put in fresh straw." Zertic was quieting down a lot. He sounded almost interested.

"Did you see the man in the car during this time?"

"No. When Goddard drove out, the car wheeled around an' folla'd him down the road."

The flashback ran across the screen of my mind. A man has driven several hours—say from New York. He's left alone near a barnyard, the time-honored rural comfort station. He takes a flashlight from the glove compartment and walks into the yard. The idling tractor engine attracts his attention. The flashlight shows him the dead horse—and, because he's an experienced horseman, the cause of his death. Zertic was muttering something. For the first time, he seemed to be trying to placate me.

"I don't know nothin' about this murder talk and I don't like it. Neither I or Jake seen the man in the car if that's what you want to know. Get me? Neither I or Jake. The man in the car don't have to worry none." He pounded out every word. "I'm goin' to tell you again so you'll understand, mister. *The man in the car don't have to worry about Jake and me!*"

I heard an automobile coming up the road where Ben had parked. Before I could duck, it turned the corner and flooded me with light—blinded me for a moment. It was at Zertic's back. The car rolled on down the road but I'd lost the man in the dark. The shovel knocked the rock out of my hand and damned near broke my wrist. Zertic sprang forward again.

"A *rock,* by God! You bluffed me with a rock!" The shovel missed my head and I took it on the shoulder—grabbed it with both hands and twisted it away from Zertic, kicking him in the belly for leverage. He grunted and backed off a couple of steps getting his balance. I could feel that he was the stronger and I wanted no part of playing pull-for-the-shovel with him. I heaved the thing as far as I could and tried to set myself for the next rush. Zertic didn't rush me. He stalked around me like he'd been watching Lee Oma in the ring. I knew he would be coming in and waited—turning, balanced always, to face him.

"You was the man in the car, Connor. You seen everything you ast me about. Now I'm goin' to take you apart."

"Don't talk about it, then. Do it!"

He made a good start anyway. When you've boxed with men like Eddie Marsh as long as I have, you forget that poor fighters lead with their rights—so I drew a sucker punch that really shook me up. Zertic's middle felt soft as I recovered and countered under his left swing. I hooked low and fast with my own left and got away. He took a noisy breath and was slow coming in again. I didn't want him to get his wind back, but I held off. Next time he got close I'd be in a wrestling match. I tried taunting him.

"What's the matter, champ? Get hurt?"

That did it. He roared in head on and I met him with all the straight, overhand right I could produce. My left wrist wouldn't take any more. The punch landed flush. Zertic tried to keep his feet, reeled back down the slope a couple of steps, and fell into the partly filled pit. I started down toward the fence and yelled for Ben.

My friend in the hole must have buzzed his way back to this sorry world pretty fast because by the time Ben drove around the corner he was bellowing for Brother Jake. As I climbed into the car a lantern started bouncing over the top of the hill and I remembered that the Zertics had no electric. My second retirement from their estate may not have been any more dignified than the first, but it was a whole hell of a lot more satisfactory.

When we got about a quarter mile down the road Ben spoke up. "Who win?"

"Split decision. Where's Doc Parkie live?"

"Maple 'n Third. You want to go there now?"

"Yes."

"You're sure you ain't got the wrong doctor? Doc Parkie's a vet." He pulled the hood off the dash lamp and looked me over. "Your face is cut up pretty good. It might want a stitch or so there in one place."

"It feels like it. Maybe Mrs. Parkie's got a needle and thread. Let's go over there."

We went. At the door of what seemed to be the Parkie home and an animal hospital combined, Ben said, "Want I should wait?"

"Yes. I won't be long."

The doorbell brought a choral effect of children, a dog or two, a short solo by dramatic soprano, and a basso aria which ended in my face when a medium big, rawboned man opened the door.

"Dr. Parkie?"

"Yes. Good Lord, man! What have you done to your face?"

"Marty Zertic did it—I didn't. I'm Connor."

"Come in, Doctor. That face needs some attention. Perhaps I'd better call Ralph Bately—"

"I'd just as soon not advertise my visit. That's why I came here—and, of course, to thank you in person for your help."

Parkie took me into his small-animal surgery and did a very creditable job of patching me up. He also prescribed and administered ounces four, Spiritus Frumenti, which enabled me to bear up with considerable fortitude. When I got to the hotel I dug out my Forester flask and, after what seemed a proper interval, carefully added ounces two.

It is just possible that the good Dr. Parkie's horse-size prescription, with my postscript, had some bearing on my behavior for the rest of the evening. In turn, I called Katie—who was out, packed my bag, checked out of the hotel, located the worthy Ben Peck parked by the movie climbed into the back seat, and said:

"Forty-eighth and Broadway."

"That'll be sixteen dollars."

19

The morning mail brought what the laboratory called a preliminary report. It was quite a production. For academic reasons, I quote from it.

". . . with negative results. Should you so instruct us, we shall be happy to make further attempts to secure a culture from the suspected material, but the fluid contained in the reservoir of the sprayer appears to be of such a nature as to render the possibility of positive results extremely unlikely . . ." Stuff-stuff-stuff. ". . . condition and appearance of the rubber bulb leads us to suspect it has been exposed to very hot water or steam for a considerable period." Stuff-stuff-stuff. "If surface indications of handling were present on any part of the device, they have been removed, either by the action of the water . . ."

I called Russ Rhodes, the boss down there, to tell him send the atomizer back and forget it. His description of the facts varied somewhat from his written report:

"Look, Doc, somebody boiled the damned thing, wiped it clean, and filled it up with glerk you could kill roaches with."

Can you beat it? That's the sort of thing that gives a guy anti-semantic tendencies!

People's Exhibit A was a dud—no matter how firmly I believed it had been the murder weapon. The Zertic horse, by this time, was a dud, too, no matter how certain I'd been of his glanderous condition. The only place anybody could turn up *Bacilli mallei,* by this time, was in the grave of Snuffy Goddard. Even there, they were giving up the hope of doing further damage and dying off. If I didn't get some action within the next few days, I'd be out (and Eddie would be in) one murder case. I called him.

"What's new on Herrick?"

"Nothing." Very snappy. "He was murdered by a wayfaring stranger. All your people at the club seem to have been working. I'm still checking. What's with you?"

"I went down to Fuldenville and got beat up."

"Hah!" His voice resounded, suddenly, with a newfound and joyous faith in the goodness of life. "Hah! Who was the lucky fellow?"

"Zertic. To save face I might add that I left him in the pit with his dead horse."

"It's okey with me, lad. It's out of our jurisdiction. Did you burn his body thoroughly?"

"Spiritually, yes. Listen, Eddie, Goddard was in Fuldenville when I figured he was. Now I want that exhumation."

"No! Sorry, but no exhumation." He said it like it had a red seal and a ribbon on it. Loud, too. "Not by my Department. That's final!"

I got a quick idea from that. "Very well, my friend, I'll get it done the hard way. I'll complain to the Health Department that the body is a menace and should be cremated. You've no idea how excited the city fathers can get over a case of glanders. Then—"

"Now look here, Doc, the—"

"Then I'll toss in, kind of casual-like, that the guy was murdered but that the boys in Homicide didn't believe it."

"Can you prove that?"

"That you didn't believe it? Sure."

"Stop talking like an idiot! Can you prove the guy was murdered?"

"I don't think so, honestly, but I can give you a better circumstantial case than most of them."

"Against whom?"

"Against the guy that killed Herrick."

"John Doe. It won't do, Doc."

"What I've got will get you a confession. I'd like to bet on it."

"You've got that much?"

"Plenty. I can tell him everything he did from the time he turned up at Zertic's farm until he followed Goddard away. I can face him with the atomizer he used to kill the man. That and more."

"So why was Goddard murdered?"

"On her account."

Eddie groaned. "Who's her?"

"That I don't know. It's something Goddard said when he was dying. Those things are not too trustworthy. I'd have paid more attention to it if I could have tied it up with anybody."

"When there's a 'her' involved, you're a chump. You're probably playing a patsy for a dame again." I waited for him to chortle and get back to the subject. "Tell you what you do, Doc. It'll save everybody embarrassment and get your corpse dug up. Call Steve Androsa at Health and tell him you have reason to believe . . . and so on. If you've got a murder, I can come in. If not you've saved just oodles of people from a death worse than Fate. I'll call Doc Androsa ahead. Swell idea?"

"It was a swell idea when I told it to you. You haven't improved it much. When do I call this person?"

"I'll have him call you right back."

"Okey. But don't let him cremate the body until they've got a positive culture or, if they can't get that, definite group diagnosis by their best men, based on thorough autopsy."

"I'll have him hold the body, all right. Stick around for his call."

I stuck around. Androsa would hold the body, departmentally, just about as long as he would hold it personally—just about as long as he'd hold a lighted bomb. When he called, I told him I had reason to believe . . . and so on.

I went out to breakfast, bolstering my confidence with the thought that I'd have a corpse to show for my efforts, even if I didn't have any murder. The corpses are the best part, anyway. Rosie peered over the counter and wanted to know what happened to my face, yet. I got the disturbing idea that maybe almost nothing had happened to it—yet. A stack of hotcakes and the morning paper proved a considerable comfort and I forgot the problem.

I forgot it for exactly thirty minutes. Then, at home, the telephone rang.

I didn't know it, but I'd been waiting for that call. Three minutes later I had made real progress—I had not only a corpse, but a motive and a conspirator, if not an accomplice.

"Doc, this is John Foster in Miami."

"Hello, John. You got something more?"

"Yes. I thought it was worth callin' you for. Your man Goddard was in Miami the day I left Palmetto Fairgrounds."

"The hell he was!" I decided I'd take my small bag. "Tell me about it. Are you sure it was the same man?"

"One of the old-timers at the track recognized him—Dad Maxwell—he's not workin' but comes around the barns a lot." I benched the small bag for a two-suiter and some old clothes. "Maxwell says he saw an ex-jock he knew drivin' a horse van with a bunch of different licenses on it. Stopped an' spoke to him when he come out the gate. Little feller, sixty-like."

"That's our man, John." I'd take my gun and have Eddie get the Florida police to give me a permit. "Did Maxwell say where Goddard was going—who he was hauling for?"

"No. I didn't think to ask him. Want I should?"

"Never mind, for now. What name did the old man use for Goddard?"

"Paddy. Paddy Goddard. Said he rode around New Orleans years ago."

"It checks. That's the right Goddard for sure." I was practically on my way. "Look, John, I'll be in Miami tonight or tomorrow morning. Will you be there?"

"Why sure, Doc. I live right downtown." He gave me an address on Southeast First. I told him to make a note of the phone charges and wound it up. There was stuff to do.

I called Eastern Air Lines, Eddie Marsh, and Katie—in that order. Each of them greeted the announcement of my proposed trip with rather positive reservations—with Eastern's by far the most practical. Eddie grudgingly promised the permit, Katie grudgingly promised to give me a chance to explain myself when I got back, and Eastern promised a seat on the early evening plane, very pleasantly.

Tomorrow morning's office hours would have to go by the board. I typed out a notice for the door. Before I got through, it was quite a thing—what with Mrs. Platt's, dicumarol instructions and Dave Zwick's Thursday iron shots. I ended it with the following: "If anybody really needs a doctor, call Perry J. Bardon. He's in the Manhattan book."

Up to the hour I left, I was unable to get hold of Pop Asher to verify the multiple licenses on Snuffy's van. Bert Mills, the watchman, had Wednesdays off and couldn't be located. Time enough for that.

By midnight I was riding down West Flagler past a lot of familiar spots—the Jai-alai Frontón, the turn to the dog track, the Columbus. From the lobby of the Columbus, I called Dick Cumming at the Towers.

"Can you bed me down for a couple of nights?"

"What do you want a bed for? Last time you were here you never used one. Come over anyway, Doc, there's a vacant stool at the bar."

On the short cab ride it occurred to me that the Towers was only a few blocks from the address John Foster had given me. I also wondered if Chick was still on the bar.

He was—with the Old Forester bottle out front, rocking, all by itself, from side to side every once in a while while Chick was apparently busy washing glasses. Even the magic routine hadn't changed. It was old home week until I remembered I should leave a call for five-thirty and went to bed.

By six in the morning I was dressed in a pair of khaki trousers and a cotton army shirt. I didn't shave. At seven I'd found some breakfast and called Foster. He said he was leaving for the track anyway, and I could ride along. I suggested he find an old pair of blinkers or something I could use to carry as a badge of my trade. He turned up at the hotel a few minutes later and I climbed aboard. In the seat beside me was a rub rag to trail out of my hip pocket and a shank to hang round my neck. Those two items are a pass to anybody's stable area in the morning.

They'd made some improvements at Southern Downs since I'd seen it. New shrubbery, gay with hibiscus, bordered the roadway and hedges of Australian pine hid the barns from trackside. Foster let me out well inside the grounds.

"You'll more'n likely find Dad Maxwell in the stands, clockin', Doc. He's there most mornin's. I'm takin' a horse to Hialeah that run here yesterday. Be back inside two hours."

"Where'll I see you?"

"Say you meet me at the back-side gate at half past nine."

There were twenty or thirty men in the big main grandstand, grouped around the spot where they could get the best shot at all the eighth poles. The works were at their peak and a horse, or a pair of them, would break from some pole or other every few seconds. When they'd ease up a little, the starter would break a set out of the gate at the head of the backstretch where he was holding school. The guy next to me said, "Ungh!" He looked at his watch and put it back in his pocket. I said, "Do you know where I might find Dad Maxwell?"

"Dad?" He looked around up the stand back of us. "Sure. That's him with the straw hat—alone up there." The guy hauled his watch out again and looked at it like he hadn't believed it the first time. I climbed up to where a healthy-looking old fellow was sitting with his eyes fastened on the stall gate, and sat a couple of yards away from him. I heard the bell go and the boys whoop as five two-year-olds left the barrier in full stride. By the time they were ten jumps away, a black head showed in front. Ten jumps more and the little black horse was all by himself. They ran three furlongs and pulled up. Maxwell chuckled to himself, then noticed me. I said, "Looks like he'd do, all right."

"He'll do till they start askin' him to run over a distance of ground. He ain't bred to go far."

"Doesn't seem like too many of 'em are these days, Dad."

He didn't seem surprised at my using his nickname. Everybody is either Dad or Pop after he hits fifty around the track. But he did look at me with a sort of quiet approval. "You're right. We run 'em too short, too fast, and too light in this country."

"You've spent your whole life with the horses, haven't you, Mr. Maxwell?"

"So far, son—and I don't see much chance of reformin' at my age." He squinted through blue eyes that hadn't needed glasses to see the colt on the backstretch. "You know me from someplace?"

"I don't think so, Dad, but I came all the way from New York to talk to you."

"Well, now, that's very interestin'. You've talked right sensible so far. Think it'll be wo'th the trip?" He gave me as nice a chuckle as he had the colt.

I showed him my complimentary police shield which, with my .38 and its permit, had been a sort of merit badge for services rendered. "My name's Connor."

"I allus got along pretty good with policemen, even when I talked myself into jail once, years ago. Right now I've got nothin' on my mind but sunshine. Who you lookin' for, Connor?"

"John Foster, told me you saw the ex-jock, Paddy Goddard, around here the other day."

"Is Paddy in some kind of trouble?"

"Paddy's dead. I'm looking for the man that killed him."

Maxwell shook his head and stared across the track. "He never was too partic'lar about the company he kept, the boy wasn't."

"How long had it been since you'd seen him until the other day?"

"Oh . . . some years, now, I'd say. I was workin' in New Orleans six, seven years ago. I think he was around then. Let me see . . . I was rubbin' horses for Tobe Jackman. Sure Paddy was around! He and a fella—some gyp or other—I forget his name—was runnin' a couple of cheap horses. Old Paddy galloped 'em the mornings he was sober enough to stick on. I seem to remember they win a race or two, there."

"Did you talk with him any when you saw him last?"

"No." The old face wrinkled in a puzzled frown. "It's funny, too. We knew each other, off an' on, for years, but he froze me out."

"Wouldn't talk?"

"Said, 'I think you got me mixed up with somebody else,' and drove down the road to the service station. It's only a piece from the gate but I was sore and didn't foller him."

"Did you notice what licenses he had on the van?"

"They was a lot of them—like most cross-country trucks. I didn't see 'em too good—didn't look at 'em until he was on his way."

"His van was empty?"

"Yes. He had the top half of the rear doors braced open for the breeze. There wa'n't any horse in the rig without he was down. He must've come in with one."

"Can you remember the day you saw him?"

"The date? Easy. It was Washington's Birthday. February twenty-second."

"About what time?"

"Close to 11 A.M. The track cops were just starting the roundup. I was going to stay for the races and was waitin' there for the roundup to get over. They always let me through if I'm around by then. It must've been right on eleven when Goddard come out."

"You wouldn't have any idea who Goddard might have been hauling for, would you, Dad?"

"No, that I wouldn't."

"Nor which direction he came from before he hit the gate?"

"Well, now, I might at that. I was talkin' with Pete Morden at the guard's box—facin' the trackside. Goddard, he come from my right. I'm sure of it. He come down from my right."

"That would mean he'd been in the north side of the stable area?"

"From the north side—and not more than two or three rows in because I had to've seen him turn to know he come from that way."

"Thanks, Dad, I think I'll look around over in that section. Where do you live? I may want to get hold of you again—if you wouldn't mind."

"I'd be glad to help you, son. I've got a nice room on'y a stone's throw from the track." He told me how to find it, then added, "If that rub rag and shank is a disguise, I'd change it soon as you can. You may know somethin' about horses, but you ain't mucked out after any in a long time with them hands. Get you a pair of sunglasses an' a camera. Then you can wander around all morning lookin' at a *Form* an' askin' questions." He made with the chuckle again. "You might even get you a tip." He walked off well pleased with his wisdom.

I ditched the disguise at the gate box and headed for the service station. A middle-aged man who looked like the owner was wiping off the pumps.

"You the boss here, mister?"

"Yeah. I own the place, if that's what you mean." He stood with his hands full of wax can and cloth. "What can I do for you?"

I hauled out the badge again. He didn't seem impressed. "A fellow who bought some service from you about four weeks ago got himself killed in New York. We want to know some things about him."

"I'm suppose' to tell you about a guy that bought something from me four weeks ago?" He made a gesture as though to go back to polishing. Then, "That's a little silly, isn't it?"

"Maybe not. Big horse van—transcontinental licenses; probably headed for New York—gates open in the rear—no horse aboard—turned out of the track gate and came directly here—jockey-size man, maybe sixty. Make any sense, now?"

"Not much, but wait a minute. What day was this?"

"February twenty-second. Washington's Birthday—about eleven in the morning."

"Maybe I can find something to remind me if it's worth the trouble."

"It is. The little guy was murdered."

He stared at me a moment. "I'll see what I've got." We walked into the glass kiosk and the man dug into a stack of sales slips, muttering to himself. He studied one carefully. "I remember the man. We changed his oil. He was in the toilet most of the time we were doing it and he didn't talk much when he came out. I can tell you one thing about him, though."

"What's that?"

"He was completely pooped out—could hardly keep his eyes open. I remember asking him where he'd come from and he said New York."

"He could have, of course—but it doesn't work with my theory about what happened."

The man grinned. "It don't have to work with your theory, mister cop—he didn't come from New York. I don't think he did, anyway. The last time he had his oil changed the service people had put a sticker on the doorframe with the mileage and the name of the station."

"So? Where had he come from?"

"If he kept his wheels on the ground and didn't disconnect his speedometer shaft, he'd come just about as straight as you can make it here from New Orleans."

I thanked him for his trouble and left—damned near getting run over as I crossed the road. My mind was in New Orleans where it all had started.

I gabbed with the man on the gate until Foster came back. The chatter was strictly off the cuff because I didn't want the Association's help until I knew what I was talking about. Racing is policed more efficiently than any other sport—and by experts.

John rolled in about on schedule and we decided to take the truck on a slow tour of the northeastern section of the stable area as though we were looking for somebody. I got the rub rag and shank and climbed on. There were, perhaps, twenty sheds on three asphalt main streets which ran north and south. The yards were between, east and west.

The tubs and buckets of some of the outfits showed familiar colors. Most of them did not. It wasn't the most desirable end of the area and was largely assigned, John told me, to the smaller strings.

Of the cars parked near by, the majority had Florida tags. Texas, Illinois, New York, South Carolina, and Georgia were represented here and there. We walked through half a dozen yards without recognizing anybody or seeing anything significant. There was a lot of general confusion as there usually is at nine-thirty in the morning—work on the track stops at nine and there are always plenty of hots to cool. The walking rings were filled and almost nobody was under the sheds. I picked a row opposite a car with a California license, the first I'd seen, and we went through at a fairly businesslike pace. A bay head—delicate, feminine and, somehow, familiar—poked out of one of the half doors along the way. I passed the stall, then turned back to look again. Before Foster could join me, I hurried on to walk with him to the end of the shed. I jittered through two more rows and suggested we call it off for the morning, but I didn't see anything I looked at. I couldn't see anything but that neat card beside the bay head which had read:

"HONOR COUNT, b.f.3—Bridgedeck-Countess Carrie."

20

Foster hauled me back to the hotel in the van. I ignored the manager's elaborate crack about my conveyance and went to the desk. Operator 9, in New York, cared to have me call her. It was Eddie Marsh.

"Listen, Doc, you'd better get back up here. I'm holding Patsy Dahl on half a dozen minor charges and Tom Bradford's in the bull pen. They damned near tore the back out of the Ricky Club last night."

"What happened?"

"Bradford won't talk—and doesn't have to, right now. Dahl claims Tom killed his partner because Herrick had found out that he has a ringer planted around the country someplace—that the horse Bradford killed—and he insists on that—wasn't Armada. Could a man make enough dough running a ringer to account for all this?"

"Hell yes, Eddie! A potful. There have been coups involving a million. Where did Dahl get all this?"

"From his girl. She'd been hanging around Goddard—nice to him, I suppose—and the old man promised her a hell of a bet one of these days, as he expressed it, if she could keep her mouth shut."

"So she trotted straight to her boy friend!"

"That's right—according to Dahl." Eddie groaned.

"Get back up here. I've got to start this case making some sense."

"It's making too much sense already. It could have been just that way."

"With Bradford calling you out to witness the condition of the dead horse?"

"Why not, Eddie? You've got to remember that Pop Asher recognized that the mare had been purposely destroyed. He may have cracked to Tom about it. Also remember that there was nothing actually criminal—in any important sense—concerned at that time. Tom would have had nothing to fear."

"I see. Where does that put Lauziere?"

"Right where he belongs. In on the deal." I didn't like any of it, but I had to consider the very logical possibility of its having been so. "Don't get me wrong. I'm not buying Dahl's story until I know a hell of a lot more about it."

"Well, dammit, get up here and find out some things! Wire me what plane you're taking and I'll meet you at the airport."

I changed my clothes and shaved, feeling pretty sour. The thing needed more time than there was. I called Eastern about planes. I could get space on a Constellation that would put me in next day around two. I had the desk pick up the tickets and wired Eddie.

A call to the Identification Bureau at the track turned up an ex-Pinkerton I'd known around New York—Jack Fullam. "Sure I remember you, Doc. I was at Empire when you cleaned up that mess Sam Eckmann was in. What goes?"

"Look in your file and see if you've got a filly called Honor Count in the grounds, will you?"

"Honor Count—Honor Count—wait a minute." His singing voice was strictly Irish tenor and off pitch. "Yes. Honor Count. Bay filly, three, by Bridgedeck, outta Countess Carrie, by Count Off. Owner-trainer, Dominick Persona . . . how much of this do you want, Doc?"

"Is she properly identified to race here?"

"Why do you ask?"

"I'm thinking of buying her." It came out fast—then stuck in my mind.

"I'm not supposed to give out a lot of stuff from this office, but hell, if you're thinking of buying her, I might as well tell you what there is to know. She's one of those cases that we're getting a lot of in the last year or so—since we started the drive for absolute identification. The horse's been raced at small tracks where they haven't got the facilities, yet, to do the kind of a job we do. Not that they're careless, but they depend pretty much on the stewards for identification."

"Which is usually damned good." I know men—stewards and professional dockers—who know thousands of horses by sight.

"It is, provided, of course, they've seen the horses a few times. The two-year-olds are tougher. There's a note attached here. Persona turned up with half a dozen horses—three of them not properly identified for racing here—and asked us to get them set. That happens all the time. We are having photographs made right now and they'll be tattooed in a day or so. I haven't a doubt in the world that you're safe in buying the mare, but that's the story."

"But the identification won't be complete for a couple of days?"

"No. We've written to Sutter Park, in California, for whatever they have on her. It's routine."

I thanked him and headed for the office of the racing papers to look at the old charts. On the way, I picked up my gun permit. Eddie had apparently done a thorough job for me. The questions were perfunctory and the boys wanted to gossip about my books.

Twenty-five minutes with the charts for the previous spring and summer gave me a lot of stuff to work on. Honor Count had been a very poor performer at Sutter—starting five times and getting nothing. Armada had won two out of three at New Orleans—one race a stake, as Tom had said. Apparently old Bridgedeck had a tendency to stamp out his fillies in a physical pattern but let it go at that. A stakes-winning mare, starting in a claimer for three-year-old maidens, would indeed be, as Snuffy had expressed it, a hell of a bet. His habit of making such remarks had probably cost him his life.

I made a note of Armada's breeder—a Mr. Jefferson May, in Kentucky—and went back to the hotel, where I put in a call for him. I also caught John Foster at home and asked him to come over. By that time I knew what I wanted to do and was damned well going to do it. Mr. Dominick Persona and I were going round and round—then Lieutenant Edward Quinn Marsh and I were going round and round.

The Kentucky call came through. I introduced myself as Dr. Connor of New York—the man who'd seen Armada the morning after her death. May was pleasant.

"I was sorry to read of the filly's dying, Doctor. Was it bad judgment in training her?"

"Not in training—but there was some bad judgment involved. Old Lance Bradford's boy Tom is in some difficulties over it."

"Lance's boy? That's too bad. How can I help?"

"Do you keep any positive identification of your yearlings?"

"Always. We're practically pioneers in identification by chestnut prints—they're as positive as thumbprints in the human—but then, I should be telling a veterinarian!"

"Would you have such a record of Armada?"

"Absolutely. I haven't yet transferred it from the active file."

"Could you airmail a photographic enlargement to Captain John Fullam, Identification Bureau, Southern Downs, Miami?"

"Is there some question about . . . good Lord, man! Don't tell me Lance Bradford's boy's got himself into a mess like that!"

"It looks like it—on the surface. I'm trying to help him."

"I'll have the prints in the mail tonight."

I repeated the name and address and asked him, for Bradford's sake, to keep his own counsel in the matter.

I was studying the data I'd copied from the charts again when John Foster called from downstairs. I felt I could trust him—and had quite a handful to trust him with. I hadn't much choice. He came in, all dressed up.

"Sit down, John. I've got to go to New York in the morning and I'll need some help from you while I'm away."

"What kind of help, Doc?"

"I think I'm going to buy a horse this evening. If I do, I want you to pick her up and bring her to New York."

"That's what I do for a living, feller. I thought you meant something—"

"I do. A man named Persona is going to sell me the horse tonight. He doesn't know about it yet, but he is. From the time I talk to him, the horse will be in danger of—let's say an accident. I'd like to have you stand by to get her away before anything happens."

"It's all legal and everything?"

"My part of it, yes. Persona's no. You saw my badge."

"Sure, Doc. I'll go along—only I didn't want to get the horsemen sore at me. They're my customers, after all."

"Persona's the only horseman that'll get sore. I doubt if he'll ever be a prospect for you again. I'm going to take you into my confidence, John. It's a ringer case—and two men have been killed over it already."

Foster looked at me quietly. "That don't scare me any, Doc. I'll do whatever you say."

After Foster had gone I composed a bill of sale for Honor Count and went downstairs and typed it on the office machine. I wired my bank and told them to stand by for a two-thousand-dollar draft—the claiming price the filly had run for at Sutter—and warned the hotel they'd probably get a call to see if I was good for it.

About the time the last race was over at Southern Downs, I called Jack Fullam again and told him some prints were coming from Kentucky that might help him—in case I didn't buy the mare—to complete her identification. He gave me Persona's hotel downtown.

Then I checked my .38 over and went down to the bar for some magic and a Forester.

At nine o'clock I called Persona's room. He said he'd be there and asked me what I wanted. I told him I wanted to talk some business with him and let it go at that. When I walked in he was civil, but suspicious. I let him have it at once.

"I'm a friend of Tom Bradford's, Persona—from New York."

"I've heard of him."

"He's in jail."

"What's that got to do with me?"

"Nothing, at the moment. I want to buy Honor Count—the Bridgedeck filly."

The man was seriously disturbed. "She's not for sale."

"I've got a hunch she will be—in a couple of minutes."

"What the hell, are you talking about? I tell you she belongs to me and she's not for sale—at any price."

"You must think a lot of a mare that can't win for two thousand in five tries at Sutter Park!"

"She's improved." He was sullen and looking for a hole by this time.

"Brother! I'll say she's improved!"

"You've had your say, Connor—now get out. I want to go to bed."

"I haven't had my say quite yet. Listen, Persona, two men have been murdered in the last month over that mare." I watched his face tighten up and go a washy yellow. "It's worth thinking about."

"Over *my* mare? That's ridiculous!" He was scared and tense. Possibly dangerous. I headed him off.

"You didn't have anything to do with it, Nick—didn't even know either of the dead men, probably." He said nothing and gave me a moment to think. "It's just possible that you don't even know that the mare you're training isn't the one you bought." He started to get up suddenly. "Don't jump around. I've got a gun and a badge."

He subsided. "I've done nothing illegal."

"That's right. I'm giving you a break rather than waiting for you to do something illegal—next time, there's a three-year-old maiden race in the book. You can take your choice, chum, between selling that filly right now for her regular claiming price or explaining to Jack Fullam why the set of prints he'll get tomorrow or next day will match your mare's."

He looked sick. "Prints? What prints?"

"Armada's prints—chestnut prints—taken as a yearling by her breeder. Get off the dime, Persona. You've got Armada and you've got no right to her. She belongs to Rick Fogan."

"These prints you're talking about—you say Fullam will have them?"

"By mail from Kentucky."

He got up and walked around the room. I didn't take my eyes off him. Finally he said, "I'll sell her to you." He stopped in front of me. "I'll sell her to you on one condition. That's that you leave me out of it."

"Who've you been dealing with, Persona?"

"You'll have to leave that out too. The question, I mean. I've been made a goat. I don't know what you're getting at but it sounds like it could be true—and I want to keep my license."

"The way this thing has been going, you'll be lucky to keep your freedom. When these two murders are properly tied up you won't have any trainer's license, that's sure. As far as legal punishment is concerned, you'll probably get away with it."

"What do you want the mare for?"

"To get her reinstated and to give her back to the man that's taken the beating on her."

He sighed and sat down. "Two thousand dollars. Is that it?"

"That's it. I'll give you my check. The Towers management will guarantee it. Here's the bill of sale."

"What about waiting till morning?"

"I'll be in New York tomorrow. Delivery tonight."

He sighed again. "Make out your check."

I called Foster to take the van to Southern Downs and hustled Persona into a cab. By midnight Armada, sleepy but thoroughly alive again, was on her way out of town.

By twelve-thirty I was in the Towers bar, watching the customers goggle at a slyly rocking bottle on the back bar.

21

On the way back from La Guardia, Eddie Marsh took turns with the siren at the business of emitting low, animal sounds whenever a car—or a thought—crowded him. I hadn't told him about buying the filly, but I'd given him the rest in some detail.

". . . but, Doc! Why in the name of common sense didn't you make Persona tell you who staked him in the deal?"

"I wanted to get back. Why should I have wasted my time listening to a lot of stuff about a dark stranger? Or Tom Bradford—whom I'd mentioned to Persona. Or Snuffy Goddard, for that matter. I'm quite certain that by this time the guy has put his horses in somebody's care and hurried to the bedside of his sick mother in Mexico."

"We might need him—"

"What for? Are you a racing investigator or a homicide cop? Within the next two weeks the guards on the gates of every track in America will have the man on the barred list."

"All right, then, who did stake Persona?"

"One of the few people in what Fogan calls his little world—maybe Fogan himself. Whoever it is will be warned—probably by now. Then I think I'll hear from him. If my guess is any good I'll hear from him before the day's over."

But I didn't.

They let Tom out during the afternoon with a twenty-dollar fine, suspended, and a warning to get himself a job and not hang around night clubs. Bradford was furious but walked the streets long enough to get the disinfectant of the jailhouse out of his lungs. It still hung in his rumpled clothing when he came in to see me. He said that he'd been to the club the night before to see Rita, who of course was not there, and that Dahl had waited until he came out the stage door again, giving him a lot of muscle-talk about ringers and a betting coup. Tom, it seems, had slugged him and, during the brawl that followed, somebody had called the cops.

"You know nothing about any such deal, Tom?" I made it very nice and quiet. He looked sincerely puzzled.

"Ringers? Doc! Are you nuts?"

"I think so, sometimes." Bradford still frowned at me. "There was a ringer, Tom."

"I don't understand . . ."

"I know you don't, kid—I never thought you did." He started to say something. "Shut up a minute and listen to me. You trust me, don't you?"

"You know I do."

"All right. Don't ask me any more questions. Go home and clean up. Then go out to the track and see Harry Knapp. He's a pretty decent sort, isn't he?"

"The best. But I can't see—"

"Hold it and listen, will you? You're back in business." Bradford fought back a flood of words. "Ask Harry if you can get temporary stall room for one horse which will be here in a couple of days. We can board the pony someplace outside for him, if it's necessary."

"*We* can . . ."

"Yes, *we*. I bought a horse in Florida and you're the trainer."

"Listen, Doc, if this is some roundabout way of giving me a break, I don't need it. I haven't come to that yet!"

"Goddammit, Tom, I bought the horse. It damned near broke me—or at least it'll keep me broke for three months. If I'd wanted to do anything for you, I wouldn't have done it the hard way. Just do what I tell you or forget the whole thing. Do you want to train for me—or don't you?"

"Sure, Doc . . . of course . . ." He petered out, got up, fumbled with his hat. "What did you buy?"

"I bought a filly called Honor Count. She ran five times as a two-year-old on the leaky-roof circuit in the West and never was close."

Bradford stared at me for a moment, put his hat on his head, and walked to the door. Then he turned to look at me again.

"Man, you *are* crazy!"

"You going to do what I asked?"

"What can I lose? Some trainers look for years for a sucker like you!"

I watched him disappear and wondered a little if the family impetuosity was getting me into another jam. The thought of getting into jams set me to composing and rehearsing a reasonably credible script for Katie. This I delivered over the telephone, giving it what I considered an excellent reading. I was gratified by her unusual willingness to listen without interruption. There was some silence when I'd finished . . . then . . .

". . . Oh! I'm so sorry, Doc. I didn't know you were through. I've been editing Monday's show since your first paragraph. Sometime you *will* tell me what really happened, won't you!"

Oh, Katie! Katie! Katie!

Then I went on waiting for the call—or the visit—or the *something* which would have to result from my Florida trip. It was close to five-thirty when it started. Maggie Marra phoned.

"Doc! Something awful is going on at the club. I thought I should call you . . ."

"What happened? Tell me."

"Danny called me about an hour ago—at home—and told me to get all our stuff out of the place. Costumes, everything. When I got there, the truck he'd called was already waiting. They've put signs on both doors—just quick ones on cardboard—saying the club is closed for redecoration and that it'll open under new management soon. There's nobody around but Lauziere and he's acting all wrong."

"How?"

"When I got there Danny was in his office—Lauziere's—and they were yelling at each other. I beat it into my dressing room and waited for them to quiet down. Finally I heard my husband walking to the front door and Lauziere hollering for him to get out and to take his so-and-so tarts with him."

"Did you see Danny after that?"

"No. I started to go out the rear to head him off, but Lauziere came through the hall, walking very stealthily, and I hid again. He bolted the stage door and then went back and put the big bar down on the main door."

"You hadn't seen Fogan at all?"

"I don't think he could have been in the building. I'll tell you why. I listened to Lauziere's footsteps and they went down the long hall toward Rick's office. Then I heard his voice on Rick's phone."

"Did you hear any of the conversation?"

"Only some of the end of it. Lauziere said, '. . . don't tell me *you're* losing your nerve! It's nothing a good dose of Epsom salts won't cure.' Then he laughed like hell, Doc. He laughed like a madman! I don't know whether it means anything."

"It means plenty. Where are you now, Maggie?"

"I'm in the delicatessen around the corner. And listen, Doc, one thing more. When I unbolted the stage door to go out, there wasn't a sound. I'm positive Lauziere was still in Rick's office, but when I closed the door and took one step away from it, somebody bolted it again. It scared hell out of me."

"It should have. Maggie! I want you to do something—right now!"

"What?"

"Go to a movie. Eat out. Do anything except go home or back to the club. Do you get me?"

"Why mustn't I go home?"

"I don't know. Just don't. I don't want you anyplace where anyone would expect to find you. You've run into something again and I haven't a very clear idea, yet, of what it is. You've been slapped around enough on account of this. Whoever hit you that night is the dirtiest kind of a killer with two murders on his hands. He won't stop at anything this time. He's in a corner."

"It sounds pretty awful . . ."

"It is awful. You can call Danny and tell him—"

"Danny isn't home—or at the office either. I tried to call a minute ago."

"All right, then, on your way—and the farther the better. I've got to go out and get myself into some more trouble."

I called Rick Fogan's apartment. No answer. Some quick speculation as to who was locked up in the club with Lauziere ended with an unpleasant mental picture of the two partners inside the place, behind barred doors, balancing the books. I called the club and, after some delay, I heard Fogan's voice—tense and quiet.

"Yes?"

"Rick? This is Doc Connor."

"Oh yes, Doc. We've decided, rather suddenly, to close the club. I'm afraid there's nothing . . ."

"I want to talk to you."

"Under the circumstances, I—"

"Listen, Rick, are you in some sort of difficulty there—at the moment, I mean?"

"Wait a minute . . ." There was a considerable period of silence. I heard the gentle thud of the receiver as it was apparently set down quietly on the desk. Then . . . "Come to the front door." The line took up its monotonous dial tone.

I debated calling Eddie Marsh and decided against it. I didn't have a case against anybody in particular and whatever I did have wouldn't call for police action. The killing of Joe Herrick was under official investigation and the killing of Snuffy Goddard was so full of obscurities that the murderer had, so far, nothing to fear from me. It seemed no time for him to start anything.

I voted against my shoulder holster for the same reasons and beat it for Broadway and a cab. I saw the crudely lettered signs as we pulled up in front of the place. The early evening was gloomy but the entrance had no lights burning. I paid off and tried the door. It was locked, so I rang the night bell. After a long wait I heard the big bar being lifted and Rick Fogan opened up.

"Hello! Come in, won't you?" He was in perfect control of himself and shook hands as though I'd just ordered the four-dollar steak and a bottle of champagne. "Sorry we're not gayer around here tonight, Doc, but I've managed to rescue some Forester from the bar." He barricaded the door again behind us.

"That's thoughtful of you, Rick. This is pretty sudden, isn't it?" We walked through the dim foyer and around the narrow hall toward Fogan's office.

"Not as sudden as you'd think. We haven't been doing too well." He swung the office door open and stood aside. "I've brought a couple of electric heaters in—the club gets damp and chilly when the furnaces are off. Sit down, Doc."

Fogan moved easily between his liquor cabinet and a small refrigerator, making drinks. Somewhere in the recesses of the building I heard a door close. Rick threw his head up, listened for an instant, glanced at me quickly, and went about his business. When we'd settled back he said:

"Now. What's on your mind?"

"What would you say, Rick, if I asked you for a bill. of sale on Armada?"

He looked at me a moment as though I'd lost my mind and then laughed easily. "I'd say you weren't the first man who'd bought a dead horse—but why do you ask that?"

"Can't you figure?"

Fogan smiled gently. "Of course I can, Doc. No man would want a bill of sale for a horse he thought was dead. You think I've been made the victim of a ringer plot. That right?"

"Yes. I don't think it, Rick, I know it. I bought Armada last night in Florida."

"The hell you did!" The man was deeply affected. He got up and brushed past my legs on his way to the door—opened it and looked out into the hall. Then he turned in the doorway and looked at me intently—his expression grave, puzzled. Finally he shook his head in a sudden, vigorous way as though to shake off the idea. I let it sink in. He said, "How do you know?"

"How do I know I bought Armada? Positive identification, Rick—from her breeder. At least that's the way I'll prove it."

"I see." He came back to his desk and sat down. "So you want a bill of sale."

"Yes. I think you can see why." He raised his eyes from the desk blotter.

"Not exactly—unless you want the mare."

"I think you know better than that, Fogan. I can't afford to own race horses."

"You're right, of course. You can't afford to own her and, at the moment—under the circumstances—I can't afford to own her either." He pondered this—sat for some time working on it. I kept quiet, listening, always, for more sounds from the locked building. If Fogan was nervous about what was going on out there, I wasn't forgetting that I was under the same roof. Before he spoke I heard a board creak not too far from the closed door. Very softly I said, "I think we're about to have a caller, Rick."

Fogan looked straight ahead of him without replying. He opened a desk drawer and took out a small black automatic. I had a moment of considerable tension until he shook his head without taking his eyes off the door. He put the gun in his pocket.

"I think not." He closed the drawer with a thump, then listened again. The board creaked. In a few seconds there were footsteps on the bare floor of the foyer. "I thought not."

"Lauziere?"

"That's right. Lauziere." Fogan reached across his desk and got a sheet from a memorandum pad. He took a pen and wrote carefully for a minute or two, read what he'd written, signed it, blotting the paper thoughtfully. "There you are, Doc—and—thanks!"

"I can't see any other way to handle it."

Fogan looked steadily at me. "I can't either."

We both got up and I started for the door. "Wait a minute, Doc." I turned. The man stepped out from behind the desk. I waited. "I have to think . . ." He hesitated, then walked to the door. Opened it. We stood there for a while without speaking. I knew he was listening.

The phone buzzer sounded at his desk and settled whatever he'd been debating. "That does it—the house phone. Go out the back way. Straight down this hall and through the dressing rooms. Wait for me outside by the stage door. I've got something more to say." The buzzer snarled again. "Will you, Doc?"

"Of course." He turned back toward his desk and I hurried down the long hall. Lauziere was calling Fogan on the house phone—probably from his office. The dim passage seemed endless and the smell of make-up was tainted with the smell of hatred and danger. I tried to listen for Lauziere's voice as I went, but could hear nothing except my own footsteps, startlingly loud on the bare floor.

At the turn in the dressing-room section, I got the wrong door and found myself in the dining room. I started to retrace my steps and heard a chair scrape as it was pushed back. I hurried through the door and into the gloom of the passage.

The lights went out.

22

I stood, lead-footed, for a minute, trying to get used to the deep gloom, listening to the traffic noises which muffled in from the outside where I wanted to be worse than a cat ever wanted kittens. I suppose the Connors have been getting themselves frightened since the first banshee howled across the old sod, but I'm willing to bet that I set some sort of a family record that evening.

My reservations about calling Eddie came back and taunted me. Maybe the killer had nothing to fear from me, as I'd reasoned, but if he hadn't, I must have scared the hell out of the electric-light company. I knew that I'd landed in the middle of a private fight, but I also had an idea that one of the private fighters was a very unpleasant kind of a murderer. If they'd turned the lights out to stalk each other in the dark, they could have it. I didn't want any.

The place, as my vision accommodated itself, took on the texture of a very dirty gray wool blanket. I could see a hole off to my right where something had partially eaten through—a crusted window, probably, and high—out of reach.

I walked toward what seemed to be the right direction for the back door. A wall guided me down a corridor and introduced my hands to a series of doors, one after the other. The dressing rooms. A pretty fair crack of light showed up forward and I headed for it. All of a sudden it blacked out and I changed my mind. Someone had walked across it. I pulled back into a doorway and listened. There was a soft, shuffled step in the hall.

"Doc!"

It was hoarse, muffled, whispered. I couldn't tell whether it was Lauziere or Fogan. I stood still and didn't answer: The sound of steps moving away told me the man didn't know where I was.

"Doc!"

Did he expect me to say, "Yes, Papa," and get shot? Fogan wasn't the sort of guy who'd run around with a gun in his hand to scare somebody. I listened some more instead. The shuffling retreated and I stuck my head out into the hall. Somebody was coming down the corridor from the opposite direction, carrying a lighted match. I ducked back and waited. Whoever it was didn't pass the door. When I'd cooked up the nerve to look out again he'd disappeared. He'd either turned back or gone into a dressing room. I didn't like it and sneaked along the wall toward the front entrance.

I'd almost made it when someone started to run through the main dining room, pounding, toward the front. A flashlight skittered along ahead of him. Other footsteps clacked across the tile of the lobby and I heard someone wrestling with the bar on the door. Two fast explosions put a colon on the end of the sounds. No footsteps, no groans, no whispered calls for Doc.

Nothing to go by—just that dirty wool smog in front of my eyes and pillows over my ears. I gave up the idea of trying to get out the front way. Somebody in the place had very strong ideas about that. I found myself at the entrance of the hall to Fogan's office and thought of the telephone. The place was black—but sooty black. I pawed along the right wall until I felt the door. It stood open.

I waited and listened.

"Rick!" Whispered. No answer.

I walked forward with my hands in front of me until I hit the desk. The telephone didn't give out with the dial tone and I started pushing buttons on the box trying to get one. Nothing happened. There was probably some other gimmick around for outside. The thought came to me that I'd pushed enough buttons to ring bells all over the joint and I'd better get out of there. I was pulling the receiver away from my ear . . .

"Who's that?" Just enough above a whisper to move the diaphragm. I almost answered when I remembered I was trapped in a narrow hall. No good. *"Quick! Who's this?"* Intense. High-pitched.

I started to hang up. The instrument rasped again.

"If it's Doc Connor, get out of here for the love of God—he'll kill you!"

The line went dead and I put the phone down carefully. It could have been either Fogan or Lauziere. It might even have been somebody else. I got out of the office as fast as I could, banging into a table or something on the way.

As I eased around the corner of the doorway my eyes—accustomed to the blackness of the office—showed me a comparatively lighter gray square which marked the lobby end of the hall. In the lower left-hand corner of the square was a black mass like a short stepladder leaned close against the wall. I studied it carefully, and earnestly kept it being a stepladder until it got cramped and moved one leg.

I felt certain the man couldn't see me, but equally certain that he knew where I was and that he'd probably heard my stumbling around getting out of the office. Whoever had warned me over the house phone a matter of seconds before could hardly have been the man waiting for me up the hall. If, as I believed, there were only three of us in the building, I had a sudden date with a killer. There was always the possibility of retreating to the office and locking myself in—which I rejected, not because I am a brave guy but because I don't like dead ends. I waited. Somewhere, deep in the building, I heard a thud like a chair overturned on a carpet—probably in the dining room where most of the chairs were on covered floor. The dark figure stirred. Turned, I guessed. Then it dissolved around the corner toward the lobby.

I crossed to the far wall and edged my way toward the end of the corridor. A flashlight snapped an instant of glare across the open door to the dining room and someone inside fired at it. I could hear the man who'd been waiting for me start to run—then saw that both men had lights. He threw a beam out front as he ran into the big room, putting a slug ahead of him for protection. They both had guns, as well.

Quiet again.

I made it to the dining-room door without incident and took up a position where I could listen and, to whatever degree the dirty light permitted, watch. Somewhere, high above, a long-forgotten skylight helped me believe I could see when I couldn't. Stacked chairs became men and an abandoned tablecloth on the dark carpet became a body. The room was damp and chilled.

I suppose that, at some time every day, there was no laughter and activity—and Olympia oysters—in the Ricky Club. You don't think much about that sort of thing unless you're a scrubwoman or a manager. But I thought of it that evening because they were staging the greatest floor show of their history—to a poor house . . .

Fogan and Lauziere were balancing the books.

There was the small scraping of a table pressed too heavily—a crashing blaze of orange from across the room as the other man shot at the sound. Another orange blob from the opposite direction and a snarling lead bee nested in the woodwork someplace. Echoes joined and roared into the rafters.

The overture!

"Lauziere!" Fogan's voice carried more impact than his slugs. It carried an avalanche of malediction that had been put together one unhurled rock at a time. Silence. Eight bars tacit.

"Lauziere!"

"There is nothing to say, Fogan."

Rick must have been deep in the room and Lauziere to my left. I was at least out of the line of fire. The bitter script went on.

"One thing, Lauziere. One thing you don't know."

"All right, make it fast. I'm coming after you."

Fogan laughed. It sounded like the rip of a belly incision. *"That statement was witnessed, Frenchie. Did you know that?"*

It had been Rick standing in the hallway. It must have been. Only one of the two men could have known I was still in the building. Lauziere fired at the voice. I heard a low cry—like a small, wounded animal—then a steady rhythm of sobbing.

It couldn't have been Fogan, yet it came from near him. He must have been startled too. The white light of his hand torch searched the wall; found the service door. There was a bright color at its edge, clinging to it, swaying with it.

Enter the star!

Rita Asher was clutching the door for support. Blood was bright against her cheek. She fell. The light went out. I heard a sound from Lauziere and sensed a fast movement—checked to a more stealthy one. I backed into the passageway behind me and headed for the dressing-room corridor as fast as the uncharted darkness of that windowless area would let me. I was wanted onstage. Lauziere's gun had written me into the show.

It was a great plot when you come to think of it. One of the two guys wanted to kill me and I had to decide which one right then. I kept on plugging toward the rear of the building. Inside the big room I heard a commotion. A stack of chairs hit the floor and a shot followed fast. More shots. More chairs down. I knew Rita must be alone and ran for it, bouncing off the wall at the turn. Someone in the dining room yelled . . .

"Take care of her, Doc . . ."

I couldn't tell who it was and didn't care by then. I got around the corner and to the service door. Rita was lying where I'd seen her. I tried to speak to her and the noise in the big room drowned out my voice. I decided she was unconscious anyway and picked her up—put her over my shoulder in a fireman's carry and headed for the only safe place I knew, Fogan's office. The ruckus died down inside—probably for more stalking, I thought. Then I realized why.

As I lugged the girl past the lobby door and into the hall I saw a heavy shadow against the gray light. Somebody was waiting for us. There was no choice and I kept on going. I tried to pretend he wasn't there but when I came to him strong fingers held my arm, words rasped in my ear.

"Into the office, Doctor, and lock the door. Here's my flashlight."

Something was stuffed into my right coat pocket and the man was gone. I bumped the girl into a couple of walls before

I made the door. Luckily I'd left it open and got her onto the desk before having to put her down. As I jumped across the room to close and lock it a burst of gunshots came from the dining room and somebody started smashing in the front of the building and a couple of sirens howled in from the street.

Enter chorus of policemen. Finale!

I bolted the door against fugitive killers and propped the flashlight over my patient. While I cleaned the mess away from what seemed to be a rather mean scalp wound, I remembered what the man in the hall had called me—Doctor, not Doc. It had been Lauziere.

Then the lights went on again and some heavy-fisted cop was pounding on the door. I opened up and told him to call an ambulance and get Eddie Marsh on the job. There was another cop standing behind him and I sent him to the squad car for a first-aid kit.

I was dabbing away at Rita's head and deciding to make sure no police surgeon put any sutures in it when she joined the party. Her opening speech was no bargain as an amenity.

"I'm going to throw up."

I chucked some flowers out of a bowl and obliged. After that she wanted to sit up and I wouldn't let her. She took another look to see who was bossing her around and said, "Hello, Doc. What happened out there?"

"You got hit. What were you doing here—why'd you come in?"

"To get my things. Phil called me to tell me the club was closing. I thought that would mean the end of the—the battling. When I came in . . ."

"How'd you get in?"

"Through the side door—we keep it for our own use. Only Rick, Phil, and I have keys." She tried to look around for the bowl again but changed her mind and settled back with a shuddered sigh. "When I got here I found myself in the middle of it. What went on?"

"I don't know yet. It was pretty rough apparently. The police are here." She thought this over. "Tell me, Rita, did you talk to me over the house phone?"

"It was you, then?" She tried to touch her head and I held her hand. "It wasn't much of a conversation. How bad's my head?"

"Not serious. No scars, either, if you get a good man right on it." She seemed satisfied with this and turned away from me on the hard desk. I stuck a chair cushion under her head. She said, "Thanks, Doc. Now let me alone a minute, will you?"

Then she cried softly, keeping it very much to herself. I thought of the challenging woman who had so enraged Katie. Then I thought of Pop Asher and Tom Bradford and, more than anyone else, Rick Fogan.

A couple of minutes later the ambulance came and I sent Rita off—with instructions—and had a chance to visit the rest of the cast of the Ricky Club's last floor show. I shoved my way through cops into the big room.

I'd have preferred a happy ending, but the script hadn't read that way. However, they were taking pictures, as they do after all big first nights, and Lauziere was posing as he had appeared in the curtain scene. He was dead on the floor.

Eddie Marsh elbowed through the group, saw that the routine was well under way, and turned to me without greeting.

"What do you know about this, Doc?"

"I think I know everything about it, now, Eddie. Where's Fogan?" I hadn't seen him anywhere.

Marsh shouted to one of the men. "Where's Fogan—the tall guy?"

"He's in the office—back there by the kitchen, Lieutenant. Pierce and Brink took him in there. They took his gun away from him and—"

We hurried into Lauziere's office. Fogan was sitting behind the desk and the two detectives were standing by the door. They spoke to Marsh, and Eddie told them to stand outside. He closed the door. Fogan rose.

"Doc! God, I'm glad you weren't hurt. Is Rita all right?"

"Yes, she'll be all right—a scalp wound."

Rick shook his head. "It was a terrible experience." He seemed to see Eddie for the first time. "Lieutenant! Sorry I didn't speak to you. Your men got here just in time."

The big cop looked at the man behind the desk very carefully. Took a good look. Then he said, "Just in time for *what,* Fogan?"

"To save my life—and possibly Doc's, here. Doc knows all about it. Lauziere told me he was coming after me and started firing. Poor Rita was hit—by accident, I suppose—then I had to fight for my life. I had faced the man with killing my mare and he went berserk . . ."

"Save it, Fogan!" The man nauseated me. "Lauziere saw *you* kill the mare and you know it. He's watched you getting yourself into trouble from the first." I turned to Eddie. "Take this guy in before I hit him, will you?"

Marsh said, "All right, Fogan, come on."

Fogan said, "This is ridiculous. I—"

I said, "If it's ridiculous, I'll take the ridicule. I could make a lot of statements here, Fogan, concerning your recent studies of *Bacilli mallei* in the Bannerton Public Library and your relations with a couple of people by the name of Goddard and Persona—but I think Lieutenant Marsh prefers more factual evidence. Don't you, Eddie?"

"That's the only kind I want. Look, Doc . . . oh well, hell! Let's go, Fogan."

I was sore. "Wait a minute. I want a look at this guy's handsome poker face when he answers this one." Eddie stared at Fogan and Fogan stared at me.

He said, "Go ahead. I've got nothing to hide."

"What I'm talking about you *can't* hide—not like atomizers and old *Racing Forms*—not like the identity of a horse. When Patsy Dahl and Joe Herrick started to prowl around because Snuffy talked too much about a big sure-thing bet, you began to lose your nerve. Then Herrick came to you and tried to sell Dahl out—or blackmail you. You sneaked away from the club at a busy hour and shot him."

Fogan gave me a supercilious sneer. "That's been a matter of police investigation, I believe. Nothing has—"

"It has been a matter of police investigation, Fogan—and the inquiry is damned near finished and you know it." The man sat very still. "When the police take a look at your gun they'll find that both Lauziere and Herrick were killed with it."

I worried like hell for a second or two. A man's physiological responses are not instantaneous and Fogan must have been fighting bitterly to control them. He opened his mouth to say something brave—and his face turned the color of death. He tried to speak again and failed. His hand, at the edge of the desk, jerked once. He looked at the walls of the narrow office.

Eddie said, "Hold it, Fogan!"

The man looked at Eddie. Then he took a deep breath.

"All right."

23

I sat in the corner of the box and watched Katie as she explained the conditions of the sixth race to Eddie Marsh and Rita Asher.

"You see, it's for fillies, three years old, which haven't won since November fifteenth—that keeps out the Florida winners, of course, because November fifteenth . . ." I don't think I've ever seen a woman look at another as pleasantly as Rita looked at Katie while she explained, not quite accurately, things Rita had known since she could read.

In two more races Tom Bradford would bring Armada across to the paddock and I was full of goodness and wellbeing. Three weeks, I find, can pass very quickly when their days are filled with Katie and Armada. My reinstatement with one and of the other had been about equally difficult.

However, the fact that neither the dead filly, Honor Count, nor Armada had been entered in a race under an assumed name made things easier—and a kind word from Mr. Fitz and Johnny gave me enough standing for two owners' licenses.

Reinstatement with Katie looked doubtful for a week, during which she disciplined me with nose and shoulder. Then I introduced her to her arch rival for my affections. From then on I couldn't keep her away from the race track and that afternoon, if she'd been interested, she could have heard herself on the air—by transcription made the day before. She assured me that she hadn't given a single recipe and had chatted about going to the races to bet on Armada.

Yes, the laboratory had been able to recover *Bacilli mallei* from Snuffy Goddard's small remains and the librarian positively identified Rick Fogan's photograph as the man who'd studied in her reference room that afternoon. Fogan and Goddard had stopped at a filling station a few miles out of Bannerton and Snuffy had crawled for several hours into one of the bunks they provide for truckers. I was mistaken in one thing. Fogan had driven back again to the Zertic farm that night for his specimen, taking the atomizer with him. The Zertics had buried the horse the next day. He'd bought a can of soup at the service-station lunch counter. That made more sense, anyway.

Lauziere, of course, had immediately recognized Goddard when he turned up at the club kitchen and Snuffy had probably said something suggestive—or even thought the headwaiter was in on the scheme, which, of course, he was not. Whatever it was, it had been enough to make Lauziere suspicious and, wanting something on Fogan, follow him to the track the night the filly was killed. I think that Lauziere must have joined in making Fogan's life pretty miserable after that.

Eddie had said we could have made a case of it if we'd needed it—which was good enough for me. There are plenty of nasty things in the papers, these days, without having to publish the utter depths to which a man can go for money.

I was brooding, vaguely, about all this when Tom's Geowaga voice broke in over my shoulder. I looked up and found him beaming at me.

"We're fixin' to leave the barn, boss, and I'd kind of like to have you walk over with us—just this time."

I excused myself and we cut our way back through the infield. The mare looked like the Queen of Sheba. Pop had braided her mane and dressed her tail in high style. The old man stood there and scuffed at her shining bay coat with his rub rag. He said, "You'll do, Mama."

Tom said, "All right, Pop, let's go."

The fifth race was going to the post as we passed the bottom of the stretch and turned for the paddock. Armada took a high-headed look and stopped—whistled a challenge. We'd drawn number 5—out of ten—and the paddock judge motioned us in.

After we'd walked awhile the valets came in and Tom saddled the filly. He was still testing the overgirth when the boys came along. I glanced at Pop as Luccino, our jock, walked toward us. Pop was staring as though he'd seen a ghost.

"Why, Doc! Them is old—" I shut him up, but Tom had caught his tone and straightened from the girth. He said, "Oh, Luccino; I want you to—"

Then he saw the colors. He looked at me.

"I thought you wouldn't mind sharing your father's lifetime colors with me. I've straightened it out with the secretary's office. You're half owner. One grand. Pay me after the race."

Tom was still staring at me when the man said, "Put your riders up."

Luccino said, "What do you want me to do, Tom?"

Bradford wheeled to the boy and snapped, "What the hell do you think I want you to do? Take this mare out to the front end and keep her there!"

Tommy Luccino told his valet in the winner's circle that day that it was the first time any trainer ever give him instructions bawling like a baby.

ODDS-ON MURDER
DANCE
JACK DOLPH

murder is
mutuel
JACK
DOLPH

hot tip
JACK DOLPH
TIP SHEET
DAILY RATINGS

JACK DOLPH
DEAD ANGEL
A.M. JAUSS

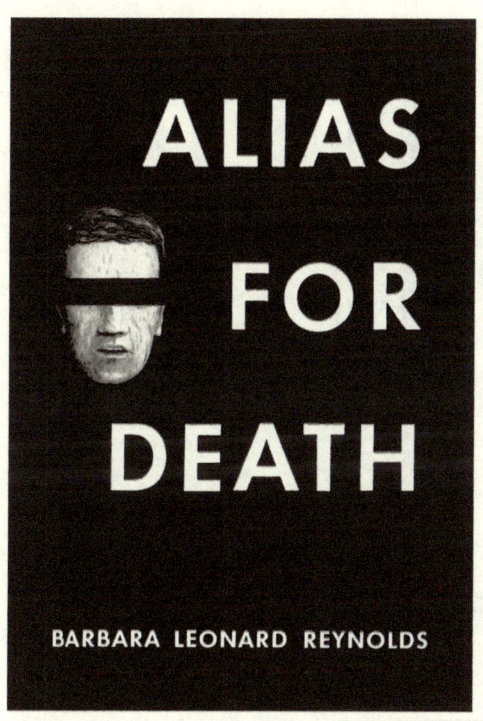
ALIAS
FOR
DEATH
BARBARA LEONARD REYNOLDS

The Serpentine Club Investigates
Murder in Washington, D.C.
THE CAPITAL
MURDER
JAMES Z. ALNER

THE FIRES AT
FITCH'S FOLLY
KENNETH WHIPPLE

FULL CRASH DIVE
ALLAN R. BOSWORTH

THE QUINNY HITE
MYSTERIES
CHINESE RED · HERE LIES THE BODY
RICHARD BURKE

THE QUINNY HITE
MYSTERIES
THE FOURTH STAR · SINISTER STREET
RICHARD BURKE

THERE IS
NO RETURN
THE ADELAIDE ADAMS MYSTERIES
ANITA BLACKMON

MARIAN
GALLAGHER
SCOTT
DEAD HANDS REACHING
DEATH'S LONG SHADOW

MARIAN
GALLAGHER
SCOTT
TALL MAN WALKING
THE ATTIC ROOM

JOHNNY
ON THE SPOT
AMEN DELL

CRIME IN
CORN-WEATHER
MARY MEIGS ATWATER

THE
MUSEUM
MURDER
JOHN T. McINTYRE

KILL 'EM
WITH
KINDNESS
By
FRED DICKENSON

www.ingramcontent.com/pod-product-compliance
Lightning Source LLC
LaVergne TN
LVHW090939080826
845145LV00003B/807

* 9 7 8 1 6 1 6 4 6 5 0 0 1 *